Praise for The Sky Changes

"As might be expected from [*The Sky Changes*] is immens~~~~ ~~~~~~~, ~~~~~ dazzling and precise verbal dexterity, and replete with both a scarcely muted sadness for the loss of love and despair over cheapened American culture."—*Washington Post Book World*

"While thematically a night journey into unholy places, stylistically *The Sky Changes* literally embodies the mind's process of change by making every detail become an incarnation of the reality presented."—Richard Howard, *New Leader*

"*The Sky Changes* captures the breakup of a marriage with brutal, arresting precision."—*Boston Globe*

"*The Sky Changes* is an odyssey of spiritual onanism, movingly and brilliantly executed."—Donald Phelps

"*The Sky Changes* is the best fiction of divorce I have ever come across, a truly moving, shattering experience." —Richard Elman, *Commonweal*

"Though its tone is dominated by despair and disillusionment, *The Sky Changes* also offers the pleasures of Gilbert Sorrentino's intense concentration and the poignancy of those few moments when redemption seems possible." —*Los Angeles Times*

"Gilbert Sorrentino is a poet, and *The Sky Changes* is poetry influenced by an insight both agitated and clear." —Gwendolyn Brooks, *Book Week*

"A brilliant, beautiful book, *The Sky Changes* strips the disguises from our misery and meanness, disclosing life to be a constant but fascinating dance of pain."—*Fort Worth Star-Telegram*

"*The Sky Changes* is not the glad, mad trip of Kerouac's *On the Road* but a bitter, more adult insight into hip America."—*Kirkus*

Books by Gilbert Sorrentino

Poetry

The Darkness Surrounds Us

Black and White

The Perfect Fiction

Corrosive Sublimate

A Dozen Oranges

Sulpiciae Elegidia/Elegiacs of Sulpicia

White Sail

The Orangery

Selected Poems: 1958-1980

Fiction

The Sky Changes

Steelwork

Imaginative Qualities of Actual Things

Splendide-Hôtel

Flawless Play Restored: The Masque of Fungo

Mulligan Stew

Aberration of Starlight

Crystal Vision

Blue Pastoral

Odd Number

Rose Theatre

Misterioso

Under the Shadow

Red the Fiend

Pack of Lies

Criticism

Something Said: Essays

The Sky Changes

Gilbert Sorrentino

Dalkey Archive Press

Library of Congress Cataloging-in-Publication Data:
       The sky changes / by Gilbert Sorrentino. — 1st Dalkey Archive ed.
            p.   cm.
       ISBN 1-56478-183-6 (alk. paper)
       I. Title.
PS3560.O7S57   1998
813'.54—dc21   97-51426
                                              CIP

This publication is partially supported by grants from the Lannan
Foundation, the National Endowment for the Arts, a federal agency, and the
Illinois Arts Council, a state agency.

Dalkey Archive Press
Illinois State University
Campus Box 4241
Normal, IL 61790-4241

for Victoria—
who knows why

Although it is not my practice to revise previously published writings, in the case of *The Sky Changes* I thought it reasonable to make this, my first published novel, a more harmonious work than the book which appeared, twenty years ago, trailing its various inadequacies. This new edition may, of course, strike readers as less than sublime, but short of a wholesale rewriting of the original, the novel is now, I perhaps fondly believe, as sound as I can make it. The revisions are not, as they say, substantive, but are for the most part intended to strengthen and purify the narrative strategies of the text. There are also added two chapters written especially for this edition which serve the purpose, one hopes, of giving the geography of the journey a greater coherence.

G.S.

And so it was I entered the broken world
To trace the visionary company of love, its voice
An instant in the wind . . .
 Hart Crane

 Divorce is
the sign of knowledge in our time,
divorce! divorce!
 William Carlos Williams

The
Sky
Changes

A Start

To discover, after 7 years, that he doesn't know her, his wife. And money available, to leave with, to go to Mexico? And why not, to face her there, break out of that cocoon that he has carefully wrapped himself in, the mummy. To look at his children, free, images of them brown and the sun hard-edged on them, chiseled out of sunlight.

Perhaps again to find her, have her come to him again, once, in the night, turn quietly toward him in the bed, and not in desperation, nor out of pity, God. To be able to say again "I love you" and not with his tongue full of dust, filth of the words, the lie, and her lie returned, to think of himself again in orgasm, not her pleasure, is there pleasure for her, was there? To be able to lie there in that sunlight, somewhere on a beach, the image of him on a beach, the heavy crack of the surf as it comes in endlessly, mesmerizing him, taking him out of his wrappings, so carefully prepared, and to talk again to her—without her falling asleep, lose all fury, all feeling of futility that drenches him as he sees her eyes go blank, she goes away somewhere, where?

Where does she go when her eyes click off that way? Not to be able to ask her, worse, not even possible to let her know that he realizes her eyes are blank. Get away from it, his house full of friends on the weekend, his ears full of their noises, away from that! Simple, then why did he not make it simple? Why ask a friend to come along, what kind of cowardice to ask along that buffer? What sort of nakedness achieved with him there, with him between them? Why not simple, why not like the voices of his children, why him to "help" them achieve a place to be, there, in Mexico?

Call him X. Call him the driver, since he drove all the way. He and the husband, and the wife, and child 1, child 2. He drove well, tirelessly, how clear, later, that it should be such an active, kinetic performance, while the husband sat in the seat next to the window, the death seat.

So the long travel, and Mexico at the end of it. He sits in the seat next to the window, so many friends to see, such a sprawling land, spattering of trees, the scenery, the country, the tearing out of the rotting roots and the firing them westward.

Brooklyn, New York

No place, it exists in *Holiday* magazine, nowhere else, or in postcards. He was born here, he strips his house, the clutter of objects there discarded, given away, his son's bike given away, his daughter's picture books. No place at all. The house empty, bitter light falling on the rugless floor, what flat anger in him, what hesitation. No place to be but worse to leave. His garden was here.

There are skyscrapers and lights and 8 million people. That's where he lived. Not a place, he lived here, he was born here, his mother is buried here, his grandmother, his grandfather, his children born here, his wife, the driver not born here. He had a garden here, bulldozed out of the earth, to build a house, the workmen stole his tomatoes, stepped on his beans, they ripped the peach trees out of the earth. His friends' vices and sadnesses no replacement, the very cracks in his alleyway shifting position, it seemed, as the shadow of the house lay on them. A poor place at best, now no place at all for him, particularly. His mother's body rotten in the ground, the plants torn from his ground, the neighbor's fig tree, grapevines hidden by the house that cuts out the sunlight, sits on the poor earth his children learned to walk on. There are photographs of him with his wife, on the limb of the peach tree, of him in his bean patch. The garden is under thousands of bricks, his son broke a window of the house with a hammer, what should he know or respect of that ugly construction? The peaches gone, the earth souring under the cement, no place for him to even sit, in the wind; go away, the light in Mexico. The sunlight. It has keen edges.

Arlington, Virginia

They are on a mattress on the floor. Their children are in a bed beside them, it is black in the room. His fingers touch her thigh, they move up to her cunt. She moves beneath them, not movement in space, but within her own body, a tension, a tightening. That he thought it would be different. What did he think, that in southern air something would happen? Or what else did he think? That in a strange house, that on the floor, that this adventure would make things change, would make her move toward him, warmly, her flesh soft? Her flesh is rigid, she is stone, she says if he wants to but the children. Howling secrets writhe in her brain, she stays rigid, what does she know, what does she want, that she cannot speak of it? If he wants to but. To say that. A kind of insanity, that is. Certainly. An insanity. His fingers are deep in her pubic thatch and she says that. Yes, he says. The voice that he hears seems to come from somewhere behind him, so that he actually looks over his shoulder. Yes, then he knows it is coming from him, it is not someone in the room, not the driver peering at them, answering for him. He moves on her, she lies quite still, he pries her lips apart with his tongue, her teeth are clenched, she opens them slightly, her hands rest lightly on his shoulders, she is still and he is pumping on her, she is still, he thinks of what he must look like, he thinks that she is thinking of what he must look like, she has plenty of opportunity to think there, so still. He moves faster, harder, he thinks that he might make her come, she does not want to come, she has turned off the switch, she turned it off the moment she lay down on the mattress. He feels himself coming, blinded with fury. What happens that he comes and it is vinegar? The spasm that shakes him is one of anger, she can't help him. She won't try, she is throttled by secrets that have fixed her someplace else. That's what has happened. He moans. She strokes his back, she feigns a move-ment of her belly, but her hips alone move. He has finished coming, he supposes. For when did it start, he cannot tell, it is almost the same, orgasm almost the same. He hears the driver turn in his sleep, he hears his children breathing. In some madness he asks her if she came. In the same madness she says no. They clutch at each other. Tell me! his brain screams, tell me! Who are you, whose children are those, tell me that which burns white in you, that turns your eyes to marble, glass. Why are you searching for my hand? His son gives a quiet cry. What dreams he walks through are no more fantastic than this searching hand. While their hearts crumble.

What? Green, rain, grey. Grey sky, grey rain, green falling apart under the fall. It sticks up out of the ground, it does not exist except as Washington exists (which does not exist except as a cemetery). They live there, people, in "projects" or their own houses. A dumb vulgarity, a vulgarity too precise in its choices to be ugly. Small in-sane asylums, of red brick, they call them "projects," or "develop-ments," or something. They squat there, they are full of government employees, they all look alike, they all look like Norman Vincent Peale, either there or becoming or going away from, toward old ex-tras' faces. It is a set filled with extras, they are filming a movie there that started with the draftsmen. Old Southern charm, the Old Do-minion. White-haired Negroes shuffle around with mint juleps, an-ger is not allowed here, the "project" committees don't like it. The supermarkets are in Colonial, but nothing is inside them except mashed potatoes to look like ice cream, blueberries in the caviar jars, tea in the whisky bottles. The clerks sweat under the hot lights. The cameras will be here any moment. Have a mint julep while you wait, please. It's really iced tea. Quite refreshing.

Who is he? When will he reveal himself? He sits and puts his sunglas-ses on, he takes his sunglasses off. He is the driver. He drives, he says that with a deprecation of his self that makes the husband pity him.

But here he comes onto home ground, he is self-mocking, but knows the area well. They are in a friend's house, the driver's friend. In a "project."

Where are the birds? Not that he cares for them, but where are they? Where are the gardens, that he cares for. Who is the driver? Where do they go when they go out? Anybody? Why does he put his sunglasses on, take his sunglasses off? His whole face changes. Not for the glare! Not at all, he won't buy that, he knows the driver isn't what he is, he changes constantly, as the light goes on, the light goes out, the sun is grey, Baltimore has laid its lash even this far, one can smell the dirty feet of East Baltimore Street, the Musical Bars. He is at home here, the husband is filled with loss, he looks at the car he doesn't drive, he looks at his belongings, he pats the canvas carryall atop the car, some of his life is hiding there. His wife wears tight pants. His wife has a beautiful body. She lies quite still more often than not. His children make him cry with love, with estrangement, he can't get through to them, anything, any more. The driver plays with them, full of gentle good humor, patience, he is his friend, goddammit, isn't he his friend? Why does he hate him when he plays with his children?

The houses are about to burst apart with boredom and deception, more will go up, burst apart. New York is north of this place. It is no place at all. But it *is* north of this place. It is really there, fig trees can't grow there, though they come out from under their linoleum and burlap every spring. They are green, they bloom, they give fresh figs. It is not a place, who says it's a place, but it is there. North of here which *is* a place and which has no birds. No gardens. It is full of Americans who hate anger and who work for the government.

Washington, D.C.

The mausoleum. Footsteps echo through the streets. They reverberate, they bounce off buildings, the streets are too wide, they are too pretty, they are long tombstones. Solemn statues confront the mowed lawns, stone lips refuse to speak, what waters are they that flow sluggishly to what sea, or bay? There are two girls in a rowboat in the middle of the river, the boat gleams against the brown water, they row upstream, past the white façades of monuments. The great spire of the Washington Monument, it gleams at the center of the city, it intimidates the city, in the slums are the Negroes, these streets are not wide, they are not pretty, somewhere around here, perhaps on the way to Arlington, is the statue of the flag raisers on Iwo Jima. They are almost all dead now?

They go to a friend's house. The driver's friend who is doing him a favor, who will forge his name to unemployment checks for 5 dollars per check. Neatly done. The husband sits in the car and waits for them to finish discussing this, he thinks, what name is really the driver's? Or is the man who is forging his name him? Who exists there? Who will come out of that house? The friend might come out and say, I am the driver and he is me, he may wear sunglasses, then how could he tell anyway? And what would his wife think? And would the friend play with his children patiently? He would hate him to do that. He waits now, he almost wants the friend to come out, he wants to go to Mexico, he doesn't want to stay here in D.C., he wants to sit in his own house again. There is a sullen intransigence here that shakes him. Or he thinks it is that. The driver comes out and they move away, turning into the broad, childless streets.

Hagerstown, Maryland

Twisted and narrow streets, almost, the husband thinks, like those in the illustrations in his children's books. Yet where are the princes and knights, the beautiful castles? Here, all is shabby, eternally grey, defeated. The people seem bent, cruelly dwarfed as if to fit the scale and angles of the town itself. Grotesque, they move slowly in the golden autumn haze. There are here no children either, that the husband can see.

They stop in the parking lot of a supermarket and load the trunk of the car with food. Somehow, they seem to be rushing, the husband drops a quart bottle of beer that spatters his shoes, the driver stalls the car as they pull out of the lot, citizens of the town stare vacantly at them. Can it be that the proximity to Washington has affected them? He laughs at himself and explains this by saying something about wasting beer. The driver smiles, swinging the car into the sunlight that turns the blacktop before them to fire.

At a roadside rest stop that commands a view of a slash through the mountains and their vast acres of fall colors stretching out to smoky grey haze, they stop to eat. The mountains are absolutely silent, the trees still. They sit and smoke and drink beer while the children throw pebbles over the fake rustic fence that edges the stop on the side where it bulges out toward the view blazing softly for miles and miles toward the west. He looks at his wife and shifts his eyes away from her. He can hear himself swallow and suddenly gets up and joins his children in throwing pebbles. The sun as it moves toward the crest of the soft mountains makes his eyes hurt. He fires the pebbles fiercely, fiercely.

Wheeling, West Virginia

The town appears suddenly, as they come off a road that has twisted up and then down a mountain, or a foothill. What the hell does he care? He squints into the sun that is on an almost exact level with the windshield, and lights a cigarette though his mouth is raw and dry from smoking.

In the sagging motel they watch an old movie on TV, Lee Marvin is a spy in a hash joint in California, or Keenan Wynn is a spy; he follows the plot fitfully, letting the whisky seep into his exhaustion and misery. Stoically, he fights against his annoyance with his wife, who is remarking on how terrific the movie is, what a great little sleeper it is. The driver agrees, they are in league, they are conspirators. When they ask him about it, he grunts, An asshole movie, made

by assholes. Who the fuck cares about movies? They turn away, silent and, he thinks, with a kind of pity at his obtuseness. He pours
himself another plastic glass half-full of bourbon and stares at the
screen. A lotta great dialogue, he says. Really *terrific*! Really *great*!

Perhaps that *is* America on the screen, he thinks, perhaps that is,
and the actors are Americans, and we are nothing at all. What am I?
Who? He is bitterly sad, bitterly perplexed in his drunkenness. That
he doesn't know a single human being in all of West Virginia! In all
of Maryland! I know you, Lee, old sport, old sock, old kid, he says
to the movie. And you are tops. His wife glances at him and puts a
finger to her lips. The driver turns the volume up a little. O.K., he
thinks. If that's America, that's America. Suddenly he has a swift
vision, absolute, of his garden, smudged greyly in the first light.
What does fucking Lee Marvin know about fucking gardens? he
thinks, and slides into sleep.

Jacksontown, Ohio

The beginnings of corn, but the land not seriously involved, concerned. A monotonous, straight superhighway that goes gently on
grades, they never heard of a hill here, and the town, off the superhighway over a blacktop, small patches of corn, horse corn probably,
Jacktown, so-called. A crossroads, a service station; some kind of
shack; a tavern; a restaurant. Then the blacktop. The town ends
suddenly at the extremities of these four things, the blacktop starts
again, goes away, into the shabby corn, the paintless houses. The bar
is called Helen and Troy's, JAX beer is sold, the glasses are iced,
Troy a drunkard, one-armed, Helen, a bustling, efficient wife. Their
daughter peers out from thick-lensed glasses. The bar is full of un-
employed textile workers, defeated farmers.

The first overt failure; the broken-down car. So the driver *can* fail,
he thinks. He chose the car, this goddamned mechanic, and failed.
It will not go. The highway is deserted, bakes in a late October sun,

the grass on the shoulders, yellowish, filled with crickets and grass-hoppers. He is drenched with a sudden despair, what pitiful belong-ings, his children sit in the back over coloring-books, is he mad? Has he lost his mind completely, what is wrong with him that he flees to Mexico, that he hasn't the strength to face his own cowardly relations with his wife at home, in New York City, where is that from here? Oh, east, they are heading due west now, the land is inhospitable, nothing grows but grass and corn, the people are withered and sun-baked like the foliage. That state trooper that picked him up and took him to—where—Jacksontown, yes. A six gun, a scatter-gun, a tear-gas gun, a machine gun, a club. The culture of the Midwest. He got out of the car once on the trip and threw a dead dog onto the shoulder of the road. How long will we be here? He wonders, where in Jack-town do we stay, there is a great deadliness here.

Eddy, the service man. He reminds him of his father-in-law, the drunk. When Eddy says that they'll have to stay at least overnight so that he can send to Columbus for the part, the husband turns away toward the shack, the night is draped on it already, the cornfields are thickening in darkness, a wind blows at him from lands he has not seen, and tears fill his eyes. His children and his wife play in front of the shack across the road, sad, still evening around them. They were to have reached Illinois by Halloween. What ghosts will prey on them here, that they have never seen? Or what will he remember that he should not? His mother rots in her grave, Eddy the service man receives her money. Let rain begin, it will! Let it drench them. He cannot plumb this misery, this land is not his. But no place here, they will be put up in a hotel in Newark. The big town. Had he known what that was, had he only known what *that* was. But there are more and more things to come, that will stab him with the grim, simple presence of their being. The driver is calm. We'll have to spend a day or two in Newark, he says. The husband gets his bag out of the car, he tells his wife. We'll have to spend a couple of days in Newark. His children ask, when do we go home? How can he tell them that not even the light bulbs exist there any more to show up the dirty walls,

the peeling ceilings, the two rooms in which love gasped and heaved
and rattled to its death? They get in a mechanic's car and are driven
to Newark, Ohio. On the way the rain begins and they get out of the
car in front of the Taft Hotel in a thin, gutless downpour. His children have never looked so ragged, his wife is shabby in levis and a
sweater, he doesn't want to think of himself. They enter the hotel.

Newark, Ohio

This must have been the county seat. They have a room, they will all
sleep in it together to save money, the driver's unemployment checks
have not started to come through. It is a big room with a double bed,
the bellboy brings in three cots. The room is illumined by one over-
head light, there is a bureau, a closet, a chair. That is all; outside
there is a short corridor which acts as a foyer and leads to the bathroom. The bathroom is almost as big as the bedroom, the tub is
huge, marble, old-fashioned. The door is wooden. They get ready
to go out, walk the town, he wants to do no more than hide from the
time that crushes him, he wants his wife so fiercely that he locks
himself into the bathroom and masturbates, his children explore the
closet, the beds are made up. Maybe we can get a drink, he thinks,
maybe we can get a drink.

Malignant clouds, black, hang on the town, the lights are on, the rain
has stopped. There is a town hall, the streets that border it make up
the shopping area, the streets outside those become "residential,"
then the whole is surrounded by the dead corn and the exhausted
earth. It is not anybody's home. State troopers drive through with
their weapons under the seats. There are huge gaps in the clouds,
weak sunlight breaking through, does anyone think that it will warm
them, any of them? The courthouse is surrounded by a plot of grass,
then a rail, then old men who stand and talk. The streetlights are old-
fashioned, there are two movie houses, there are other things equally

ugly, the town festers in a kind of fantastic ugliness, a dream land-scape. In the very center of town there is a huge hotel, the windows are boarded up, the doors are ripped from their hinges, inside is a smell of must and rat shit and death that oozes out onto the street, and people pass it by on their way to the movies as if it is not there. Perhaps it was built that way, for character.

Jacksontown, Ohio

Columbus doesn't have the part, Eddy says. They have to send for it to Akron. Another day or so, folks. They all laugh. Does Eddy know that one more day will be the end of his marriage? Does Eddy know that? Does Eddy know that his wife's eyes are turned inward almost all the time now? That she doesn't hear him when he speaks to her? That it has got to the point at which he nags her about her smoking? Does Eddy know that he would like to take her into the abandoned hotel and fuck her amid the putrefacting rubble and the millions of rats, their eyes edged with filth? Does Eddy know that the driver has a name that no one knows, that he thinks, himself, that he is someone that he isn't? Where is Akron? In Mexico? It is Halloween. They don't mention it to the children, they thought they would be in Illinois, they thought that the kids would be able to duck for apples and the rest with their old friends' son. There isn't much of that simplicity in anybody's life and here, they miss it. They are in Newark. Well, another day, folks. Got to send to Akron. You can always have a couple of beers over to Helen and Troy's. They can. They do. Troy looks at his wife's ass in the tight levis when they walk in, and whispers something to the farmer next to him at the bar. They both laugh, the laughs, beer, and snot churning into one thing in their throats. Beer, and cokes for the kids, just a couple and then we'll be off. He doesn't know that it will be another two days.

The outhouse behind the tavern is a nightmare. Spattered with shit, soaked with piss, but no obscenities on the walls. Troy's cock is

lodged firmly in his mind, it drips on the cerebrum, he has a cerebel-
lum covered with chancres. There are no obscenities on the walls.
One slips on shit on the way out. From the door is a view of the fields
beyond the crossroads. Corn stalks stick up in *rigor mortis*.

Drakestown, New Jersey

1939; 10 years old; a farm. "I'll Never Smile Again." Hitler march-
ing. He sees up a girl's skirt for the first time, she is wearing pink
pants, she is about 16. Her sister is 18, she has a date, she goes dancing. The date's car has a radio playing that tune. A soft night on the
Jersey truck farms, beautiful land, it rolls and dips, the barn sounds
of animals settling for the night. He walks behind the house to the
outhouse, the smell is good to him, rich and heavy, the boards are
scrubbed clean, the night leaping fast over the croquet lawn. His
grandfather plays in the twilight, he wears knickers, soft lights.
Sweet music. The fields are rich, a bull bellows far down in the hollow behind the copse of birches. He inhales, the girl whose pants he
saw is singing, "until I smile at you." His mother is going dancing at
the WigWam tonight with Tom Elwood, he would be a good father.
Would he be a good father? He has a mustache, he smokes a pipe, he
is handsome, strong. It is 1939. A great innocence enfolds them, the
farmer can still grow rhubarb and sell it fresh. He can sell his own
eggs, fresh. The milk is brought to the table foaming, pasteurization
is scoffed at. The milk tastes of sweet grass. Across the road the old
white church is chalky in the light. His mother is calling him, he goes
out, she stands on the edge of the croquet lawn, in a white dress,
white shoes. She is indistinct in the gentle darkness that enfolds her.
Tom Elwood is in his car. His radio plays the same song, that was a
popular song that year, 1939, nobody knew that the words were for
all of them. His mother's voice calls good-by. The moon leans on the
steeple, crickets are beginning in the raspberry patch.

Jacksontown, Ohio

Driving rain now. The blacktop glistens in the headlights, the fields moan to November. The sky is nowhere, is there a sky here? Leaning farmhouses are back in that mud, that moving silt, boards soaked through, lamps through the windows spill out light but the fields are dark, occasionally a profile of cornstalks against a square of light. The rain sweeps from the west, into it.

They leave at 1 in the morning, absolute desperation has jumped on him, he cannot wait, let the kids sleep in the car, if they drive all night they can cross the Illinois border by 9 or 10, the kids are under old army blankets, his wife back there with them, he and the driver face the road, he glances at his profile occasionally, he is growing a mustache, he notes. That edges him closer to an obscurity, that changes him further, hair by hair. Oncoming headlights cluster thick near Columbus, through it, through it. Illinois in the morning, goddammit, and sunlight? Pray to God for it, pray to God that it will knife through this corpse of autumn at the border. But first Indiana. Is it anything like the mood of that old tune, he wonders. It's there ahead, out in the slashing rain. Those lights ahead must be Columbus. Sign: JACKSONTOWN 32.

Columbus, Ohio

Something dismal is handling him; not the lights of the cars, not the town coming up fast. Is that his wife back there, does he recognize her at all? Are they his children? He doesn't play with them any more, what a stupid reserve he has with them. And with her. It would serve him, justly, if she were to get out here at this light and leave. God, the guilts that strangle him. This fucking town, what a perfect name. Columbus. After that failure. The usual car lots. The usual drive-ins. Nobody in the streets, police in the streets. The Midwest is made up of police and drive-ins. Pinch-faced car-hops.

Their whole hearts full of alum, secreted into the blood. She won't get out here, she would die here, his children would be swept up by the wind, the rain would dissolve them. The farmers would use them all for fertilizer. Farmers! What do they know about farming here, they stick the seeds into the black soil and breathe on them and they have their 500 acres of corn, which they burn, or throw to the hogs or plow under. If you take an ear to feed ducks or chickens, they have the police on you. Tight souls.

She *will* leave the car, get out at this Cocktail Lounge, go into the bathroom and leave by the back door, never return, her voice will probe his ear forever. You made me go, you wouldn't even ask why my eyes were marble, why I touched you as if you were not there. You accepted it, why do you love me so much that you cannot ask me, one thing, one question, why are we going to Mexico with him, why did you allow us to sleep all together in one hotel room, like animals, our souls and hearts twisted and writhing against each other? Can't you be nicer to the children? Can't you take them out once in a while? They're around me all day. All day. All day.

A nice town, the driver says. O.K., he'll accept that without comment. Though he feels as if he is moving through hell. Mists rise from a cemetery. No, it isn't a cemetery, it's a street where the better citizens live, the lights are hooded, the driveways are aglitter with vehicles, the windows burn warmly with the glimmering fires of brilliant conversation, the greatest minds in all of the United States are here in this Columbus, he can feel it, he can sense it! There is nobody in those houses who would drive his own children through this bitter rain, covered with army blankets, dreaming about home.

He reaches back to adjust the blanket on his wife, and her hands are freezing. Or are they his hands that are freezing? He cannot tell. Anything. Any more. Be in Indianapolis at dawn, the driver says. Great orange signal flags break from his mouth, he cheers loudly, the rain whirls and pelts around them. His garden lies under tons of cheap bricks, it will never grow again. And what of all the friends that walked down that alley, between the lot and the house? What of them? There is a deadly crawling in the hair at the back of his neck. He scratches as if to kill lice. What of them, those visitors? Why didn't I ask them to leave with me, when I left in the morning for work? Did I think or imagine things that might have been true? They are not true, we are on our way to Mexico to buy leather handbags, letter openers with *Recuerdo* on the blades, that's all. Sit on the beach, the driver will disappear into the sea. Why haven't I learned to drive well enough for a license? Why haven't I that one escape hatch? Is this the damned Foreign Legion? His wife's face is shattered into pieces by the lights which slash through the car, her expression seems to be one of exhaustion, or she is two women. Or three? Where is Indianapolis? What are those fingers there on the black horizon? Westward.

Indiana

The clouds. From the top of the sky, dark, but light against that incredible darkness that holds them. That holds the land. Corn there on the left, the right. Corn before them, behind them, exists in time, almost, they create it. They go through it, dead, dried stalks, they are creaking in the wind. The clouds fall in streamers from the sky to the earth, they stretch across the land in front of them, they will run into them and through them and then the sky will be clear. Gigantic fingers they are now, he thinks, what fingers, of God? Of Satan? Some incredible power. Or bars? They don't want humans to pass them, they don't want to give up their west, they are fingers dripping blood, they shape the sunrise from that direction, they curl under the earth and push the sun up over its rim, in blood. The dead cornfields, the clouds are forbidding.

Or towns. Hopper paintings, barred store fronts, an anonymity of evil, there is no life behind them, there is nothing on the streets, they are drowned in a glare of fluorescence, and nothing moves on

---

---

them. At the very edge, the edges surrounding, the dead cornfields. Crackle, the clouds are visible through the blinding light. One wild migratory duck waddles in the street before a barbershop, his green neck glitters in the light, he moves. They move. The town lies still as these things move against it helplessly.

New York, New York

In white, suitable. White slip, panties, brassière, garter belt, shoes. Stockings a misty flesh. She takes a bath. She sings. No, it is a shower she takes. She sings. "It's Getting to Be a Habit with Me." He smiles. He is a man. He has a wife, he takes the chilled white wine out of the refrigerator, he stands wrapped in a towel.

It fell out of his hands somehow, didn't it? How could it happen that it fell out of his hands? He remembers the night his son was conceived. Of course. Does he remember it, all the couplings were ecstatic, then.

She comes out of the bathroom, naked, he swallows, offers her some wine, and they drink, they drink more, everything she says interests him. They finish the wine and he opens another bottle, they finger and fondle each other, they fuck, once, twice, three times. The third time she calls him by another name and his heart shrinks to a plum.

Indianapolis, Indiana

Something macabre in the air here, the town as if gripped by the Mafia, or some other blood lust. It shivers in the grey dawn hurled up to the sky by the fields around. There are people taking buses, there is an old Negro waiting on a corner for the light to change so that he can cross the street. He carries a lunch bag, spotted with grease, his shoes are run down at the heels and the soles are broken, he sways in time to some grief inside him, it's for the whole town.

White buildings splashed with the nondescript light ranked around him and his cohorts, both white and colored, as giants, sentinels, so that they cannot leave. What kind of city is it that stands in the center of a thousand miles of cornland?

The driver knows some way out of here, some way back onto the highway that will avoid the early morning traffic. Oh, he is knowing, he has been through Indianapolis before, he has been to Mexico many times, to Europe twice, walking through Europe, broke. Why would a man want to walk through Europe? In blood and corpses up to the ankles there. Bad enough here, though perversely, the rawness saves it. And then it comes to him that perhaps the white buildings are not that at all, but grain elevators. What does a grain elevator look like? He remembers photographs of them vaguely from an old grammar school geography book. They don't teach it any more in school at all. Nobody wants to know where anything is, any more. Too many dead bodies lie in places nobody ever wanted to go. Is it strange or not that his father lives in a city he has never seen? The sunlight begins to make the car headlights useless, people flood into the city over the highway, as they break out again into the beginnings of the great flatness that is, for all he knows, what the rest of the world is like. They stop for coffee, in a clean, all-night coffee shop that is sort of a better-class White Tower. His wife stirs, his children sleep on, very peacefully now. This fact, that they are dreamless and still, gushes an inexplicable happiness through him, his undefined griefs are assuaged.

Illinois

You can't tell the difference between this and Indiana, that is the difference here. Should there be a difference? Why not an absolute change, as of color, or shape of trees and foliage, when you cross the state lines? Or, perhaps, the corn is taller, certainly the earth is darker, darkest, almost black. It is like humus. Glows with blackness. The road signs are great green squares with the towns and mileage in reflector letters. The sun glints their fame at you from a quarter mile down the road.

Now they will see S and B and their son. He teaches in a town here, Urbana, where the University of Illinois is. Pray God that the children don't remember Halloween, now. The road is too straight, the sun is bright enough to anger him. The people move around underneath it, they don't look up at it, they move, on tractors, hulking, irregular forms of red and yellow and green, buzzing in the sun, hornets, beetles, in among the dead tan cornstalks, plowing it in, under. The driver comes from this state, though farther south, not cornland, God knows what kind of land. When they get there, perhaps they will have their own room, perhaps S will see what gross error he has made in this fanatic journey, and give them a room, alone. Though what good that would do, he doesn't know. The children might not wish a room of their own, they might cry at night for her, and she would have to go to them, or something would have to be done, wouldn't it. But someplace in the house where they could lie down at night and not hear his breathing a few feet away from them. Or what is wrong with *him*, the damn driving son of a bitch? Why doesn't he insist on being away from them, what kind of voyeurism compels him to accept whatever bedding arrangements seem best? The hell with what is best, go somewhere where it is not comfortable, at least one night out of 5 or 6. But that night, she would turn and say: it's too planned, I can't when it's too planned, I have to be spontaneous. And he would believe her. What happened to that chilled white wine, and the rest? What happened to his aggressiveness? It is as if he suddenly, one night, became one yearning question, one gigantic erection begging fulfillment. And her avoidance, the endless falling asleep on the couch, the TV programs that ran too late for them to do anything, but sleep, for he had to work the next day, worked while guests came to see her, he blenches at that, a bitterness purses his mouth, he can almost hear the flesh tearing at that ugly memory, which he allowed. He was as passive then, as the driver now. And with no good reason at all, did not at all do what was best, suffered the impositions and went to work, the good old skate: he thinks with bitterness. He glances at the face, the sunglasses fixed on the road in front of him. Brother. To Urbana, we can all feel superior there, since S and B slash at each other constantly, a necessary slashing. He doesn't yet know that the ugliness must surface as scum or else it poisons the innards, the very entrails. The sun is well up now, his daughter wakes, smiling, the sun holds her face, a gentle effulgence. His son wakes a moment later, and asks: where are we? He can tell the boy that they will be at S's for breakfast. So. Things are possible, again, the night is gone, the rain gone. The children have stopped asking about home.

Urbana, Illinois

They do many things here, get drunk many times, they have liquor stores here that carry every possible type of alcoholic beverage that can be sold. The farmers get drunk in the neighboring town, the students and instructors get drunk here. Nothing to do but drink. S as nervous, as strident as ever, thinner perhaps than he was in New York, shaking apart with tensions, his wife honed to a razor edge of frustration, they flood the visitors with questions of New York.

What they do, S and the husband, every day, is take the children across a little stream and into a park, with trees and artificial hills, there are no real hills in the entire Midwest, by his reckoning. They come with corn picked up in the fields at the edge of town, half-eaten ears that the reapers have missed. They bring it for the ducks, but there are geese also. S hates the geese, why, he cannot say with any clarity, but his hate is real. On a cold and brilliant day, they stand, S, the husband, the 3 children, at the edge of the pond. S kicks in a maniac rage at the geese who come crowding and honking forward with the ducks, picking and ravaging at the kernels that they throw, the children shout and scream with glee, short-lived. What moral to draw, or why does it so burn itself into him: the fact that S fashions a spear out of a tree branch, sharpens it to a needle point with his pocketknife, fires it with all his strength at one of the stupid, flapping

geese. And hits him well, hits him hard enough so that the spear stays
in his gross body, just beneath the wing, he convulses in pain, the
other birds swim madly around him, the children are stilled, S's son
says: he was a bad goose, daddy, he was a bad goose, daddy. The
husband's children are dumb with fear of the violence. S is white
with anguish, he keeps saying to the husband: he isn't really hurt,
he's just stuck a little, there's no blood. There is no blood, but the
sight of that tortured goose, that ignorant bird, splashing the still
water of the pond, the other birds paddling and crying around him,
the stick goading him, hampering his movements, is enough to make
the husband sick, though he smiles at his children and tells them it
was all a joke, S really just scared the goose, you can't hurt geese. S
watches the wounded goose splash down around the shore, out of
sight behind a little island, or outcropping of earth. They throw
handfuls of the corn into the water, the ducks and other geese come
back, and eat, and crowd, and shove at each other. The husband
suggests that they ride on the swings, the children. They leave the
shore and walk through heaps of crackling leaves, a bitter wind
drives clouds, blinking out the sun again and again, there is a feel of
frost in the air, a feel of deadly winter. Behind them, the birds jostle
for the last few kernels of drowned corn. They walk in silence. Cruelty surrounds them, the children are changed in his eyes, the ob-
scure misery that hurts them, though they have no word for it, is
guilt. S and the husband have full awareness of it. Their guilt. S's
act, the husband's inability to say even one word to him, or better
yet, splash into the water and pull the torture instrument from the
hapless bird, the children swing against the greying sky, no more is
said, they are in the center of the United States of America and their
host is a college instructor. In the humanities.

Belleville, Illinois

In southern Illinois, the more urbane and cosmopolitan members of
the town like to think of it as a suburb of East St. Louis, or St. Louis
itself, the other members of the town apparently don't think about it

at all. But it is better than Newark, Ohio, at least seems better to him, although perhaps that is because it is the driver's home town. They see his old house, the house in which he was raised, the "block" he played ball on. The husband is amazed at the huge white house, the "block" is more a road, just half paved, hedges and trees glutting its borders, the traffic is almost nonexistent. He thinks of his own child-hood, the small apartment, the bare concrete street, the 10¢ a day his mother gave him during vacation so that he could buy lunch while she worked at a steam table in a cafeteria. There is of course the omnipresent town hall, the post office, the main street with movie and 5-and-10. But he feels that he has a chance here. At least a chance to see the driver at home, see him as a reality, instead of "the visitor to New York." The walker through Europe. And there is hardly any corn for miles around, the earth has gentle dips and rises, trees and other foliage.

When they arrive, the driver goes to see his father at the real-estate office he works at, and meets him in the street, just leaving the office. They greet each other as if they had seen each other at breakfast, instead of what is actually so—that they have not seen each other for 4 or 5 months. He would like to believe that his own upbringing was filled with embraces, huggings, kisses, at renewed acquaintance-ships, partings, that this flatness is new to him, unreal. He thinks that perhaps the driver and his father are at odds, and watches for more revealing signs of this, but it is, the driver later assures him, the way they have always been with each other. Pals. This might have been a clue to many things which later took the husband by surprise. Definitely an indication of nonidentity, which, instead of being strengthened in the husband's mind by this meeting, was more or less changed to become what he thought was the driver's strong "front" to hide his emotions. This he understands, being somewhat guilty himself. But the driver does not have this front. This inability to respond *is* what he possesses, it is no mask. But here, at this mo-ment, in Belleville, the husband accepts it as the unwillingness of two men to show their love for each other out of a feeling of embar-rassment.

The evening is spent in the driver's home. They sit and drink tall bourbons with soda and ice, and the mother and father talk of the Church, and Father this, Father that, the K of C, the driver's early altar-boy pictures are shown along with pictures of the house, the old house, the family in Mexico, in Europe, in South America. The children sleep upstairs, quietly. They are getting used to the no-madic life, they seem to be either enjoying it, or they are too stunned by it to understand just what is going on with this constant traveling. A sister and her husband enter, they chat, they recall old times, the brother-in-law and the driver talk in oblique references to "good times" in New York. The evening ends in animated discussion of an article on surgery that appeared in the *Reader's Digest*. Everyone participates except the husband, who drinks steadily and uncom-promisingly, and the wife, who smiles at everyone and everything. The next morning they are packed and ready to go, south into Mis-souri and Arkansas, then Memphis. They leave in cold rain. He thinks, if they could get out of the rain, drive out of it, perhaps things would change for the better for him and her, thinking, as he settles in the death seat, of her quivering tension, the tangible disgust of her body with his the night before.

Southern Illinois

They travel on Route 66, and the husband sings whatever words of the old popular song he can remember, the land begins to lose its sparse lushness and turn into red clay, mounds and heaps of it mak-ing up road shoulders. Wherever they drive, in whatever direction (now toward the south), they seem to head into clouds, into rain, as if even the weather is trying to tell him that the whole thing is stupid. The one thing he did not really know is that it would be stupid. He expected nothing in particular to change on the road, but he did not expect it to be stupid. And it was that sort of stupidity that turns in upon itself and becomes painful to see. An arrogance begins to well up in him pertaining to all this dead land, this wasted heartland, the grim, set people who inhabit it.

Urbana, Illinois

Picking ravaged ears of corn with S, the land stretching away to nowhere, in every direction, and a fierce wind worrying their clothing, S leaping about insanely in the field, jerking his head up, bird-like, to see if the police are coming, or the farmer, or whatever terrors are uppermost at the moment in his mind, half drunk, both of them, the children crackling among the waste of stalks around them, searching also for corn. And the wind blowing steadily from Canada down upon them, nothing but trees and fields to stop it, nothing but that and the people bent against it, to stop it, for 3000 miles. A debilitating futility seized him, the wind was aimed directly at him, as if to freeze his heart. Suddenly he straightened up in fury, loss was the single emotion he felt, loss, lost in this howling wind. S leaped on, babbling, clutching at wormy corncobs, speaking maniacally of the choruses of Euripides, a swollen gesturing toward madness; he stooped again, searching in the rows for yellow.

New York, New York

They had gone to the party late, he, his wife, a friend (the driver, now). He was up that weekend from D.C. and they had finally got a baby-sitter. The party was uptown, held to celebrate the birthday of P. P was the lover of his best friend's wife, but the husband did not know this, nor did his best friend. A stupid, drunken party, full of the misfit rabble from the edges of the art world. They had read some books and made fun of Eisenhower, so they felt that they were different. The whisky worked in him, he wanted simply to get high, feel good, but he drank too fast, he was stinking and then he was suddenly dancing with his best friend's wife, as soon as he took her in his arms he could feel her body notch its contours into his, she was drunk, laughing, and they were dancing to an old chase record of Wardell Gray and Dexter Gordon. C's record. C's wife. They sweated profusely, grinning at the other dancers, his own wife was off somewhere, he did not know where, he did not, this time, care. C's wife was throwing her belly against his groin, he was blind with desire, her lover was there somewhere, grinning at someone, holding a monkey, his eyes myopic behind his thick lenses. Great bubbles of laughter formed in him, broke in him, he did not laugh aloud, however, he was silent, he sweated, he felt the sweat stinging his eyes, it was magnificent, thrilling, his life, its shackles were cast from him, the woman was a talisman to drive away his guilt, his need, assuage his burning lusts. What would C say, if he knew. He did not know, he would not know, surely no one would tell him (dancing, stumbling across the floor). They were in a bedroom, his back against the closed door now, the dark around them, and somebody shouted outside for beer, or fear. He pushed her to her knees, and she did not protest, she giggled heavily, fumbled at his fly, it was heaven, fuck him, fuck him too, fuck my old lady he thought as she worked her mouth and tongue expertly and he slouched against the door, smiling stupidly into the darkness, contemptuous of the idiots outside the door, grinning, grunting, in relief, lust, but mostly in gratitude.

Arkansas

The car, the goddamned car, was losing oil as they sloshed along roads that threaded through grim red clay fields, drenched in rain, some were almost lakes. Negro cabins, grey, paintless, stood here and there, faded flowered curtains, cardboard, torn sheets over the windows, probably to blot out as best they could the impossibly desolate fields around them, rice fields, cotton fields, all long harvested, here and there, floating in the scudding water that covered the road, a grey boll, bobbing and heaving on the swift, tiny waves that the wind pushed across the slick macadam. They were losing oil by the quart now, and Memphis was over 40 miles away; occasionally they passed "towns," occasionally they passed motels, but the car

was definitely in such bad shape that it needed the attention of a
dealer. He hated the driver now, hated him for his expertise, his
knowledge that the car was irreparable except for the equipment of a
large garage. And hated him for the failure of the expertise that had
been responsible for choosing this car. But the husband had allowed
it, had asked him to buy it, had wired him the money, over 500 dollars, for this lemon that pulled them into only rain, unrelenting
grief. He had left a stable misery, a possible misery, to find the same
misery on the road, and rain, and the driver drove, he had removed
his sunglasses now, the rain fell in sheets, the children sat in the back
and looked out the windows, they fought, his daughter whined with
boredom and his guilt tore at him. Memphis, Memphis, where the
dealer is. And more money to be spent on this car, more of his rotting
mother's money; how his grandmother would have laughed to know
how this money was being wasted, how it had brought, so far, only a
floundering, and a stupid groping for happiness, away from that city
that the money had been earned in, grappled for, starved for, that
city where his grandmother had created a hell into which they had
all been cast, to amass this money, that now was being spent on oil,
a quart every five miles, two quarts, and the roads swimming in
brown, driven water, the bedraggled fields with their despairing Negroes, the cotton gins, huge machineries of endless money-making
every few miles, and rice plants. His grandmother would have
laughed, laughed. She, too, rotted long ago, in the ground, next to
his mother. A travesty of justice to see his mother's coffin go into the
grave next to that woman who had made, who had spent her life
making, one perfected hell into which the shattered family all were
drawn inexorably, into which his child's life had been plunged, in
which he had been made to feel the guilt of their collective sins, their
niggling, their cowardice, their impossibly cadaverous relations with
the life surrounding them. The rain lashed down; he thought of
all the—what did he want most when a child?—candy, cookies, all
the things, food, that was it, food . . . he thought of all the food that
could have been bought for this money, thought of all the food that
could have been bought for the blood, the dextrose, the care and pills

and knowledge pumped and poured and forced into the putrefacting, malice-ridden body of that woman, who now, out of her rotten earth, surely laughed. They would make Memphis, the oil poured into the gasping engine profligately, keeping alive this used machine; whoever had used it? Had he been happy? Had he taken his children on a long and desperate journey away from the unalterable, but pathologically ignored fact that his wife was not in love with him, had never been in love with him, had found with him only bitterness and want, that his wife was to everyone else she cared for those things she was not to him, a lover, a whore, *even* a wife? He had used the car to go to the beach, and to work, to go bowling. But Mexico was beautiful. What he would not admit to himself was that Mexico was his hazy memory of drunken weekends spent in whorehouses and bars, laughing, free, griping about the army in which he was, he knew, though no one else did, a willing prisoner. They were going to stop at an unlikely café for Mexican food but the children complained, they revolted, and he gave in to them, as he was doing more and more often now, feeling that they had a right to their small desires and dislikes, who had been so ruthlessly torn from what they knew, but he did not, was home.

Memphis, Tennessee

A city of used-car lots and garages, beaten Negroes, shabby whites. Small parks, each with its green Confederate hero, spattered with birdshit, swords held high, huge-rumped war horses charging toward red and white, blue, yellow FOR SALE banners cracking in a yellow breeze. These statues, these heroes, are not simply incidental decorations, they command each small park, the parks are created around them, nothing learned in the north can be of use here, they are all living someplace else, they believe in these dead men, the attitude is one of sanctity, of preservation; holding on to something that was, when vital, useless at best, now it is all beyond even that, the uselessness. A heavy despair in the very rays of the November sunshine—they feel, here, that things might have been different had they won the war. How they still wish that the darkies were gay, and not struggling for a right even they are not sure *is* a right. The Mississippi powerful, the perimeter of half the city, brown and mighty, hardly moving, far off down-current, a seaplane lands, a pencil line of silver behind it as it silently knifes the river with its pontoons, it taxis, turns into the wind, gathers speed, takes off again, the children watch, fascinated, the three adults sit in the sun, watch the river, walk, sit, smoke; there is little to do because it is a Thursday and they may not enter the museum or the zoo—it is Negro Day in Memphis. He feels that nothing he has ever learned is of value here, that all would be met with a smile of Southern toleration, feels, worse, that whatever he has learned is not only not helpful, or useful, but a concrete detriment. The driver looks through his sunglasses, looks over his thin mustache, at the river. He makes some kind of comment about it, the tone of voice is intelligent, the husband smiles politely and returns the vapidity. His wife smiles distantly, she looks as if she would like to be on the plane. He remembers reading a pornographic story once in which the heroine is fucked by the pilot over the ocean, reaching orgasm as the plane runs out of gas and plunges into the sea. Just before they crash she tells him that he is the only man she has ever loved, as she sits astraddle him, impaled on his phallus, the terrifying dive into oblivion curdling their guts, their mouths pasted together, or, as the word read, "patsed" together.

The car is not simply in bad shape, it is in desperate shape. The clutch is gone, the crankshaft is split, the engine has been ruined by the forced 40-odd-mile drive through the wastes of Arkansas to reach Memphis. The dealer smiles and says that he can give him top value in a trade-in on a new car. The husband feels that everything is now closing in on him, these impossible occurrences urge him to simply run away, go back, but he smiles back, he asks if there is any alternative, and the dealer consults the mechanics. They say that a new engine can be installed in two days, at a cost of a little under 400 dollars, and he says, almost brightly, O.K. They go, as gypsies, again carrying their suitcases, into a hotel down the street; the clerk looks at them suspiciously, obviously vagrants, or transient workers, something must be wrong with them, dressed as they are, with a broken-down car, here in Memphis, city of light. But they get two rooms, he is almost embarrassed as he gets two rooms, feels almost as if he is slighting or betraying the driver, who stands, suitcase in hand, holding his daughter by the hand, his wife behind him with his son, a dark-blue spring coat over her sweat shirt and levis. What a rabble! What a lost rabble. He feels nothing but shame as they follow the Negro bellboy to the elevator, he smiles, smiles, wondering desperately about whisky, he must get drunk or he will crumble.

Brooklyn, New York

The husband is unloading 375 cartons from a truck, thinking that it's Thursday, and only one more day to go, and then the weekend— he hopes that F will still be there when he gets home, and that he'll stay the weekend: he won't, then, feel the blind, stifled rage toward his wife that he feels when they are alone on the weekends, and he tries desperately to get her drunk, arouse her passion. Occasionally they do make love; she stares away into the blind corridors of self-pity and he dutifully grinds away at her still loins, staring, also, down his own corridors of self-pity, worse, self-doubt. Wherever it went wrong no longer matters to him, they move in a bleak world of shadows, nuances, half-assertions of unhappiness. But the children! After all, the children! You can't just leave, walk out on the children. He fires a carton onto the flat drawn up to the trailer-box, the sweat reeking on him, the clock moving inexorably on.

New York, New York

The husband lies still on the couch, not wanting to disturb C and his girl, next door, in the bedroom. He knows, at a far remove, that the lumpy couch he lies on was once his, the same couch that held so many guests and lovers, betrayers and freeloaders, friends still known and the nameless host of drunkards and pot-smokers who spent years—aeons—of time in his house, sucking out of him what he once thought of (seriously) as vitality; the nights of entertainment, the small room jammed with people, from Washington and Texas and Canada and Europe, all day, all night, the money so sweated for gone into booze and food for the locusts that descended to laugh at his lies, his elaborate stories and to ogle his wife, fuck her if that was possible, and he knows now, of course, that it was possible many times. And now the couch that he thought he would never see again, that he and the driver lugged up the stairs of the tenement on the lower East Side, to give to him, C—C, now divorced from his wife, the same emotionally debt-ridden girl who had feverishly and totally accepted him in the maelstrom of that party, now so long ago. The same couch, and his friend in the next room, with a girl, the weekend just beginning, and the husband back in New York now, with some clothes, some books, the rest of his mother's money neatly noted in a bankbook, and minus his wife, his children. But he had his couch back, and for a blanket, a chenille spread; the wind howled outside, the snow thick and spastic in the courtyard, far away across the land traversed just months before, his estranged family with the driver, man and wife and children, the masquerade played out for the benefit of the good residents of San Antone, Texas. He tasted what he could have sworn was turnips in his mouth, the room swam, he discovered he was drunk enough to puke, and sat up, hearing C's low laughter from the bedroom, leaning his back gently against his one-time couch. If it weren't so goddamned sad he thought, if it weren't so goddamned sad . . . he suddenly threw up on the floor, between his feet, noticed that he still had his socks on.

Gallup, New Mexico

He sits on the toilet in his roomette on the Santa Fe Chief. He has diarrhea, and his hands are shaking, there are beads of cold sweat on his forehead, and he drinks from a pint bottle of Jim Beam, gagging as he swallows. A crevice of sunlight appears at the side of the window shade at the moment the train begins to slow, entering Gallup. Carefully he puts the bottle on the floor and peeks out through the window, the shade pulled slightly back. New Mexican sun floods into his eyes, dazzling off the red sand and sterile mesas of rose and blue in the distance, the patches of powdery snow milk-white. The soft gong of the diner steward approaches along the corridor, and he thinks, I should eat something. He picks up the bottle and drinks again, gagging again, choking, then retching bile and whisky onto the floor, his eyes still fixed on the buildings as the Chief shoulders quietly into the yards. Down an embankment sown with snow and rocks of blue and rust, the Log Cabin Motel; he starts as he sees what appears to be a green Ford station wagon in one of the carports, covered with dust and silvery rime, then as the angle changes he sees that it is a Rambler, but he keeps staring at it, staring at the motel as the Chief picks up speed, then staring at the ruthless land lavish before him. A drop of sweat hangs from the tip of his nose and his guts begin to flop over as the Chief hits its stride clattering and swaying toward Albuquerque.

Memphis, Tennessee

The rain that they had run out of, quartered away from as they plowed through Arkansas, has now caught up with them, and it streams down the hotel windows as they sit in the driver's room, the children asleep in the adjoining room, both of them in the large single bed, exhausted after the half day of standing and waiting around the garage. The husband has bought a bottle of bourbon and they have a bucket of ice and a pitcher of water; they sit, drinking and talking, avoiding the subject of the car as best they can. The driver feels responsible, he says, for not having realized he got a lemon: then the conversation takes another direction. The wife goes into the other room, and 15 minutes later comes out dressed in a suit and coat, high heels and stockings. She smiles into the thin air that now seems to surround them wherever they go and tells her husband that she is going out, to walk around the town, she wants to see the town. He begins to protest, but then realizes that it doesn't matter to him one way or the other; whatever controls he may have had over her life are all ineffectual now, all of them without any base of operations save for the malfunctioning station wagon. There is no stability that he may hold to, no place he may stand from which to speak, he drops more ice into his glass, and she comes over to kiss his cheek, say good-by to the driver, who looks at her hungrily, amused, his eyes quietly resting on the curve of her buttock and thigh, sipping his whisky. She turns to leave, and as she does, the husband suggests to the driver that they play a few hands of gin, wanting to roar out in surprised anger and self-pity at this absurd idea. The driver is willing, so they begin, after the husband checks to see if his children are still sleeping. He fantasies: the wife crosses the lobby and goes out into the rain to see if—yes, he is there, a rather tall and skinny man of about 45 or so, in a rumpled gabardine suit and a trench coat, his hat dark with water, outside the hotel. He smiles as he smiled when they entered to register, and turns quickly to walk down the street past the Ford dealer, around the corner to his car, the woman a half block behind him, her feet wet already in the heavy, solid downpour. She opens the door and gets in beside him, smiles, laughs then, then accepts the flask he offers. You're a real pretty woman, the man says. She smiles again, drinking. A real pretty woman. They embrace frantically then, seeking each other's groins, groping, insane with lust. This is how, she thinks, this is how, an adventure! A great adventure of the road! The foulness of his breath is obvious beneath the smell of peppermint as she tugs dutifully to free his phallus. I only have about a half hour, she says.

Drakestown, New Jersey

He had fallen asleep listening to the cries of birds he had no name for, but somehow wordlessly designated as "country birds." He dreamed of Tom Elwood, surrounded by the odor of the delicately perfumed pomade he used in his hair, the rich and delicious smell of his pipe tobacco; he was dressed in white and held him in his arms and a woman he did not recognize, but whom he knew to be his mother, was standing with him. They were all flipping War cards, he had what seemed like millions of them, all of them that he ever wanted, and Tom Elwood kept buying him more from his grandmother, who stood nearby, scowling—but she didn't dare refuse Tom Elwood, and she didn't hit him with the leather belt that swung from her hand. He heard his grandfather's voice saying, is that you, is that you, and he was trying to say, it's me Gramp, and then he was awake, and he saw against the grey square of the window the figure of his grandfather, leaning out, calling loudly the dream words, is that you, and then, come up here instantly, and he knew, suddenly, and, although he did not realize it, bitterly, that his grandfather was talking out the window to his mother on the road beneath. How could his grandfather talk that way to his mother, who was so big, who was his *mother*? He heard the click of the gate latch and after a few moments his mother came into the room and he heard a muffled argument, then a sob, as he feigned sleep. He wondered if Tom Elwood would be nice to him. He had nothing to do with how his grandfather acted, did he? The next day his mother's face was cold and set hard, and she merely nodded to Tom Elwood, then a day or two later he realized that Tom Elwood wasn't there any longer. He spent his days alone, down in the fields behind the cow barns. Once he licked the salt block that he discovered there, and wished he were a cow. When, later, he asked his mother about Tom Elwood, she told him that they wouldn't see him again, that he already had a little boy that he had to take care of. He didn't cry, he simply wandered through the fields, missing the baking streets of the city; he liked it here, but his grandfather was always telling him how lucky he was that he was off the streets for two weeks, how much better off he was than the other boys who had to stay in the city all summer. He used to be able to take this sort of thing, but now, all he could think of was how old and cruel his grandfather looked, he didn't like him at all. His mother never spoke to his grandfather any more now, just at the table when everybody sat for meals. His grandfather sat in the evenings on the church steps across the road. One night they had a bazaar in the weed-grown yard of the church and he was allowed to go across the road and buy lemonade and play the wheel of fortune, once. Then he came back to the house, took a bath, and went to bed. He thought of Tom Elwood and began to cry, soundlessly. Since he had always slept in the same room with his grandfather or his mother, or on a couch in the living room, he had become expert at this. It gave him a bizarre pleasure to feel the tears, hot and tickling, running down his cheeks and into his ears. He squeezed his eyes tight shut and his mouth formed the word, sonofabitch.

Memphis, Tennessee

There's no sense to it, none at all, so I'll stop trying, it's too much for me. The utter degradation of asking, and fumbling, with the smile affixed to the face, as if the whole thing is a little game. A little game, but we always know who'll win. Let me read, please, I'd like to finish this book, besides, is that all you ever want out of me, just a fuck? He does well by now, it's happened so many times, he does very well, lying with his back to her, feigning sleep. The book she reads is one of pseudo-pornography, *Good Time Girl*, or *Brute Desire*, or *Lust of Beasts*, with the heroine on the cover adjusting her garter, a square-jawed blond faggot in the doorway. And the children sleep quietly across the room, the driver also asleep in his room, he guesses. The husband rises and goes to the bathroom, yawning extravagantly, and stumbling against a chair. He sits on the toilet and masturbates, thinking of himself and his wife in the act of fornication, sodomy, all variants that he can imagine. In a spirit of what can only be called revenge, perhaps contempt, he thinks of her with the driver, how would she be with him? Has she ever had a chance with him, he wonders, then thinks of that night, election night, in the motel in Missouri. He forgot all about that. They had a chance there, to at least play around. Guiltily, he realizes that these thoughts are making him hotter, but he doesn't stop, he doesn't want to stop, fuck

her! Serves her right. He has reached the precise psychopathology
of believing that he is inflicting shame and pain on her by thinking
her into degrading situations of his own invention. Serves the frigid
bitch right, he thinks, and comes.

Missouri

Between Belleville and the red clay and floods of Arkansas lay the red
clay and harsh hills of Missouri. Endless single-lane blacktops and,
of course, the rain. Jesse James country. They take the children to
Jesse James' Hideout. The cave that the gang used has a shoddy
restaurant and gift shop built against it.

For some reason he refuses to investigate and discover, the cave
terrifies him. The fact that the bored guide with his flashlight and
rote patter is embarrassing to him does not negate his terror. The
children are awed, looking at the stalactites, the underground river,
the pools, the natural causeways and paths. Where Jesse James di-
vided up the loot from the so-and-so robbery, where he did this,
where he did that, and two wax figures to represent Jesse and another
of the gang, protected by a wire-mesh fence, brilliant under a powerful spotlight. The figures fill him with horror, they seem to smile
at him, they are waiting for him, for his soul and blasted life, they
have been waiting for years, these ghosts, this cave, its black, hidden
waters poised to receive him. He feels that he has entered his hell,
that he has been vouchsafed a glimpse of it, here on earth, his spot,
his particular *bolgia*. The nuns used to tell them in religion class that
if they could see the pits that were awaiting them in hell, awaiting
them if they did not remain in the state of grace, they would never do
evil, commit sins again. And the worst places were reserved for those
guilty of the sins of impurity, in thought, word, and deed. The dev-
ilish wax figures watched him as they followed the guide deeper into
the cave, cool, damp air blew from the blackness before them into
their faces and he thought he was going to be sick. What could save
him, what acts must he perform to prove to the guardians of this hell
that he was a good man, that he had always done his best, that he was

trying, even now, to remake his life? It was his wife, she was the one, she didn't understand him, she didn't love him, she stared into voids he could not plumb, her eyes were blank, were marble, so much, so much of the time. She wouldn't love him, and he squandered his manhood to avoid arguments, felt it slip away from him daily, for seven years it had slipped away, a little each day, her fault. Give me a break, he thought, and then laughed at himself, damn fool, a couple of fucking wax figures in a tourist-trap attraction. Don't miss Jesse James' Hideout while in Missouri! The figures stared blindly past the wire mesh, into the recesses of the cave, the black water flowed mysteriously, rushing to freedom—where was that?—beneath his feet. He shivered in the unaccustomed dampness.

They had to get off the slick blacktop as soon as possible, the rain and the two-lane road making the driving hazardous, the woods crashing in the downpour on either side of the moving car, trailer trucks battering headlights at them as they rounded curves or swept quickly over the crests of hills, but they wanted to find a good motel, they'd already passed two or three that were run-down, rain-drenched unpainted cabins, all seemingly empty. Although it was unspoken, the three of them were intimidated by this weather, it had followed them all the way from Ohio, they needed some sort of "luxury" to compensate for the feeling that they somehow deserved this wretched rain, so they looked for a place where they might rent a room with a television set, a place where they might shower at leisure, have an iced drink or two, cheese and crackers from their supply of food in the insulated chest. To stop, get off this road that the car swayed and skidded on, no matter how carefully the driver maneuvered, a fierce night.

Memphis, Tennessee

The car was ready, the day brilliant, the rain had finally deserted them completely, it seemed. It was Armistice Day, and Memphis was beginning its annual parade, just as the car rolled out of the

dealer's garage. They drove around the city for hours, each turn
leading them to a motorcycle police detail or a foot patrolman who
directed them down a street where another policeman would direct
them down a street, until finally they were back in the center of the
city, no possible way, it seemed, that they could get out of Memphis
until the parade ended; the city fathers apparently never considered
that some heretic few might want to leave the city, therefore all traffic
directions led vehicles from the outskirts into the center of the city.
At last, they found a motorcycle cop who told them that one street
was being employed for another half hour, at least, for outgoing
traffic, and they got to it. Rather, he, the driver, got to it, with his
uncanny sense of direction, his ability to function in the traffic of a
strange city as if he had lived there all his life. The husband sat,
looking out of the right window at the parade preparations, his wife
next to him, the children not even asking if they could stay to watch
the parade, so sophisticated and jaded had they become—or so it
seemed to him. Had this been, or, better, was this to be what he had
finally done, his ultimate sin? To completely rob his children, his
lovely uncomplaining children, of their childishness? The driver
turned down the proper street and gunned the car as a cop waved
them through almost frantically. Another five minutes and they
were passing bars, gas stations, and bowling alleys scattered here
and there along the highway, and they were past the city limits.

Missouri

That's the part he forgot, or didn't, wouldn't think about. Of course,
they had a chance there, in the motel. While he, like a fumbling idiot,
hiding his rancor, kept walking down the row of cabins from the
driver's cabin to theirs, to see that the children were all right. They
took turns. How bitterly he said that to himself, "turns." Because
marriage is a bargain, right, and life, well, life is just a bowl of pie in
the sky, right? So they would take turns going from the cabin down
the row to look in on the sleeping children. The driver had a televi-

sion set in his cabin, and they watched the election returns, drank from a bottle of Cherry Heering they had somewhere, for some reason, bought. No ice was available unless they wanted to go down the road a mile or so to a machine and the roads now were almost impossible to drive on, the rain accompanied by fierce blasts of wind. They had an excellent chance each time he was gone, to fondle and kiss, didn't they? Why should he think of this? Whatever else she was she was faithful. She had to be faithful, the only people who would have had an opportunity with her were all his friends, and they were really friends, they were good friends who came all the way over to Brooklyn to see him, chat with him, all the way from Texas and Washington to talk over old times in the army, talk, talk, good friends with no reason to cuckold him, and besides she wouldn't let them, would she? A good wife and mother, even if she didn't love him. She was at least, faithful. She respected him. For what, he wondered.

Mississippi

Out of the rain and deeper into the sunlight, all the brush and weeds along the road tangled with cotton bolls, and endless fields of cotton. Storms of cotton as gusts of wind slapped across the fields and along the roads, and pickers, bandannaed, straw-hatted, bent, far away; in the center of each field a ramshackle wagon into which the bags are emptied, bending, picking, each remote from the other, working in this still-hot November sun, whites and Negroes each to their own field, even in their sweaty, aching poverty, apart.

Is it possible that he has found out the secret? What secret? Not, after all, a secret at all, but he remembers now what F told him long ago, that is, maybe two years ago, sitting in the back yard at dawn, drinking gin and orange juice for breakfast, the sun pale and the air cool and still, they spoke quietly, not wanting to wake the neighbors, the drinks were delicious, icy and tart. F had said—he was writing a book of short stories at that time, and he tried to talk many of them out before working—he had said, he has no back: I mean, he has no back at all, I mean, he's flat, straight as a plank from his neck down to his ankles, you can't trust a man like that. An assless wonder. I'm going, he said, taking a long pull at the drink, to write a story about a man like that, he's going to be the villain; sort of a fiendish Dr. Nirvana, like in Captain Marvel—matter of fact, I'll call the story "Captain Marvel," Captain Marvel will be a nice guy like me—or you. They laughed, and the husband went quietly into the house, made two more drinks, and came out again. Don't, F said, don't ever trust a man in a pair of pants that won't hang close on his ass. You're drunk, he said. Of course, what the hell. But don't trust Captain Nirvana, I mean, Dr. Nirvana. He thought, now, the great sovereign state of Mississippi passing on either side, does that make him a villain? F is right, he has no back, no character at all in his back, I mean from the rear. Nothing, anonymous. But that's probably from sitting behind so many wheels, driving so many thousands of miles, he has worn himself flat, his back left in a thousand Fords, on a thousand beds in Youth Hostels, on ten thousand friends' couches. He lost his back a - trav'lin'. Left it beneath a million free European stars. He looked slyly across at the driver, who drove on, mustache fuzzy, his back and seat almost a right angle with the cushion.

They drove into one of the small picnic groves off the highway, much like the one they had stopped at outside Hagerstown. One of the many state-owned "oases" that one sees across America; they include covered wooden picnic tables and benches, small fireplaces, and trash cans. Their provender was neatly arranged on one of the tables—beans, pickles, frankfurters, hamburger meat that his wife made into patties. Beyond the clearing of the grove stretched a sparsely wooded area, knee-deep in parched weeds and grass, a slight freckling of shade from the few birches and pines against the still, hot, green-brown of that vegetation. The children played in the small field, the boy swinging around and around the trunk of a slender birch, the girl leaping and falling, rolling in the hot grass. The husband built a fire in one of the cement fireplaces, one that was shaded by a tree, the driver gathered wood from the field, and from the other fireplaces, chunks of half-burned faggots, pieces of charcoal. The car glinted sun from its green sides and top, the fenders and lower doors thick and dull with red clay and mud.

A state trooper's sedan pulled into the grove and stopped. The door swung open slowly and the young trooper, faceless, dressed in grey to match the color of his car, stared out at them. He pulled his hat down over his eyes, then slouched behind the wheel, narrowly surveying them as they made preparations to eat. He made no motion after he slouched, he said no word. Twenty-five yards away, just behind their wagon, he watched calmly. Perhaps there is something suspicious about us, the husband thought. We are obviously not propertied, we are obviously transients, the out-of-state plates (New York plates!), the canvas carryall, the shabby stained clothing. Definitely improvident. And one woman with two men, none of us Southern. We are here to blow up Dixie! We are here with black bombs to destroy the fabric of the genteel South! Anarchists and Reds, nigger-lovers from New York! The trooper watched; the husband built the fire up unnecessarily, glancing up obliquely as he worked; the driver stood with his back to the sedan, dropping another armload of wood by the fireplace; the wife opened beans, stripped labels off the cans so that they could be placed directly into the fire; and the children played, not caring, truly ignoring the trooper. He senses something wrong with us, the husband thought. They began frying hamburgers on a flattened tin can formed into a makeshift skillet, nervously joking, not daring to glance at the trooper, waiting to hear, any minute, the sound of his boots on the gravel, and the patient, drawling voice, Where y'all bound for? but it didn't come, and they ate, quickly, prodding the children to hurry. They drank coke, although they had beer in the car, in the cooler. Perhaps there was a law . . . ? No one said a word about beer, it was simply not necessary, they felt a momentary warmth toward each other at their mutual recognition of a possible danger. But maybe it was against the law to build a fire, to stop here, to be from out of the state of Mississippi? Perhaps this trooper knew of immoral acts to come, things no one now knew of, knew that this woman and this backless man, this flat-assed man who bit voraciously into a hamburger, would allow their lust for each other its freedom? Perhaps he knew that the other man, the older one, was enmeshed in his hopeless role of bystander, even catalyst? If he knew, he would do something: the husband sensed all this, then looked, frightened, was it really a trooper? Who *is* in that car? Is that the waxen face, the petrified grin of Jesse James? They were packing their food up, carefully, almost methodically, throwing their rubbish into the large cans marked RUBBISH MISSISSIPPI DEPARTMENT OF HIGHWAYS, then they were putting things away in the car.

They heard the door of the trooper's sedan shut, and the starting of his motor, then he backed out of the grove onto the highway and moved north. The husband settled into the car with the others, pinched the leatherette case holding his traveler's checks, the money that stood against all of Mississippi law: that's why, he thought, irrationally, he knew that this money is from the dead, against all of them. But somewhere deep in his brain he assumed that the trooper had known something far different, had asserted himself as an agent, demonic and unreal as the wax figures in the cave. It was as if his whole life were being watched, each mistake, each lie now, might be the one to ruin him. But he laughed and joked about the "cracker bastard" as they headed (and he was relieved) south, toward Jackson. The children ate cookies and drew with their crayons as the car plunged in and out of shadows.

Oxford, Mississippi

They decided to detour 30 miles or so that they might pass through Oxford, and see the university, and the country of the Snopeses and Sartorises; the drive there was unmarked by any event but for seeing an occasional car bearing students toward the university or from it, each flying its pathetic little Confederate battle flag from the antenna. The episode of the state trooper back at the picnic grove had created a spurious warmth among the three of them, they talked aimlessly, pleasantly, as the car moved along over the empty roads, the deserted cotton fields stretched on either side, so incredibly Southern, as if the country had gone out of its way to plant these fields not for itself, but for out-of-state tourists, so that they might know it was truly Mississippi. The husband didn't like any of it, he sensed some kind of subtle sadism in the very air they passed through, a long history of blood and darkness disguised in the warm breeze and brilliant sun that enveloped them. He remembered a Southerner he had met his first week in the army who told him of the tree in his home town that had been used for lynchings so many times that there was a groove worn into its lower limb. He saw in his mind the wide, yellowish face broken into a grin, the front teeth split to make an inverted V. This was that same country, it was not the land of grand Biblical tragedy and despair that had been written of, so grandly and despairingly. The cruelty was neither tragic nor grand, it was simple and diurnal, in its very vulgarity it was terrible: abject Negroes walked the roads, their heads in bandannas, occasionally an old man or a boy sat a horse or broken mule. They seemed lifeless, crushed, they were concrete symbols of this country that had sullenly slashed its own throat and called the gesture magnificence.

They were in Oxford, then, a brittle picayune sore of a town, baked crisp in the sun and covered over with a haze of dust. Flat two-story buildings composed themselves in a square around the blistered and peeling ugliness of the courthouse, the stone Confederate soldier stared out through the dust and glare at what the townspeople all believed was lost glory. An old Negro woman with the right of way at a street crossing glanced quickly at the car as it moved toward her, saw that the occupants were white and painfully backtracked to the curb so that they might pass first. This was graciousness. They drove about the university grounds, and the husband felt that he was on a stage set. Whatever might be learned here? Let's get on the road, he said. This whole place gives me the creeps. Unbelievably, he missed the raw fertility of the Midwest. This dusty lushness smelled of blood. The car moved back through the town, and toward the highway to Jackson, the Confederate soldier glared out over the harvested cotton fields with the identical eyes of the state trooper at the picnic grove. They gained the highway and headed South. With any luck at all, they would make Jackson by about 9 that evening. The driver had an old friend from college who lived there with his wife and children, and they planned to stay with them for a few days. The sun blinded his eyes as he turned to stare at the sudden dazzling whiteness of a crumbling but newly painted cabin at the edge of the road. The Negroes on its porch stood against the white, clear as steel engravings, staring at the car.

San Francisco, California

He was in a bar, terribly drunk, and yet his mind seemed clear, and precise in its thoughts. He knew that he hated all these people clustered at the bar and jammed together at the tables, shouting at each other, fags and dykes and an assorted bouquet of artistic types. All he wanted to do was get into bed with one of these chicks, he thought. He ordered a drink and saw that he was sitting next to a blonde dressed in a sacklike garment and sandals. It's January, he thought, sandals? and said, excuse me, are you a German, from your accent, I mean? He noticed as she turned to him that his drink was gone, and he ordered another drink, and drank that one in an instant and ordered another one. She said, in a friendly way, no. He touched her back and said let's get out of here. He was suave, he was moving fast, it was like a movie, he imagined. He felt that he wielded total power over the situation, then a young man, well dressed, said, watch your fuckin hands, you creep, and he said, fuck you, you tourist prick, and the young man hit him. He felt himself strike the floor, and he scrambled up, then lurched against a table and knocked it over, then fell again, among spilled drinks and broken glass. The bartender picked him up and pushed him out the door. He turned to go back in and the bartender straight-armed him, which seemed amusing, he shouted 24, 46, hike! and rushed the door again, and the bartender

socked him. He went down, got up again, and walked across the
street; after a minute he walked into a bar that was empty but for a
fat businessman and a whore who huddled together at the end of the
bar, chuckling. The fat man held one of the girl's breasts in his hand
and swayed back and forth on his stool. He fished in his wallet and
took out a 20, put it on the bar, and ordered a beer, trying to look
prosperous and dignified. The bartender came over to him and
looked at his torn shirt and the blood on his chest and face, and said,
out. He got up, forgetting the 20. He decided he might as well go
home, that is, back to Q's house, if he could find a cab. Suddenly he
was filled with anger, this fuckin shitheel town, 2 o'clock and you
can't get a fuckin cab. He sat down on the curb, then remembered
his 20, got up and went back to the bar. The bartender glared at him,
and pointed to the door. Get out you bum or I'll call the cops. My 20,
he said. You fuckin bum, the bartender said, and vaulted the bar, are
you tellin me you left money in here? My 20, he said, and as he said
it, he gave up as his brain lost its clear edges and turned to mush. He
felt himself stumbling through the door, the bartender behind him,
shoving, and fell again on the street. He got up and started walking.
Gotta get back to the apple, he thought. Boy, have I been out of
circulation. Suddenly he missed them terribly and would have cried
except that he knew that would make him feel better, and he treasured up his misery carefully. Back to the big apple, he sang, and
began to truck down the street, laughing furiously, his misery trans-
formed to an almost uncontrollable manic exultation.

Jackson, Mississippi

They were so used to lying to each other that they never realized that
they were; that is, they could discuss those failings, or apparent failings, in others, things that were also their own despair, as if they
themselves were thoroughly free from guilt. So, they talked that
night in bed of the hostess's obvious problems with her husband.
They were right about her: she was a woman whose nerves were

stretched so taut that she seemed about to begin a kind of actual humming, as plucked guitar strings. Her problems were a compound of various tiny miseries, the most potent of which was a loss of faith in her husband's manliness, the least of which was the neat little one-family house they lived in on the edge of that grim and puritanical town. He thought, as they almost smugly discussed her and her husband, I could make her with ease. As he recalled the beautiful soft bulge of her buttocks beneath her slacks and the way she stabbed nervously at the air with her cigarette, her lips drawing back from her teeth in a death's-head grin, tense, he got an erection. He fumbled for his wife and she, in a panic, tried to roll away from him, yawning ludicrously. But he had to have her, and he sprawled heavily over her body, suddenly delighted, thrilled, so that his breath came raspingly out of him: she was hot, violently passionate, biting, heaving, clawing and moaning as he socked it into her. For a moment he thought that he would prolong it but it was impossible, if he didn't come, now, he would screech. She held him to her achingly, whispering nonsense and obscenities into his ear and he knew that she wasn't thinking of him at all, it was anybody, anything, a rod of stiff meat was her beloved: what pleased him so is that he didn't mind at all. His great pleasure was that he felt as if he had triumphed over the driver, who slept tonight on the living-room couch. It was sheer triumph, the feeling that a man may get when he cuckolds his best friend, his most trusting friend, by seducing his apparently totally faithful wife or mistress. Triumph in Mississippi, thinking, as he fell off to sleep, 1000 miles between fucks. After he fell asleep, his wife reached orgasm by masturbating.

He offered to make supper the next night, boasting about his magnificent spaghetti sauce, and everyone agreed that it would be great to have it. The host complained that he hadn't had any Italian food at all since he left Chicago even though Jackson had some "Italian" restaurants: which led to jokes about Jewish spaghetti: tomato soup over pasty macaroni, and if it's really daring some fried green peppers thrown in. He and the hostess went into town while the rest

stayed home, and they chatted, amicably. He was surprised to see
her so calm as she drove, it acted almost as therapy for her. Each time
she stopped for a light she began to get nervous, but when the car
rolled forward again, the woman was in complete control. He looked
at her with utter lust, and formulated a hundred insane plans to
seduce her, somewhere along the road—or perhaps a motel, but he
simply smoked and talked of his amazement that two Northerners
could live in such a town, and she told him how it was the only fairly
open, hence, lucrative territory her husband had to choose from in
his job as a meatcutting-machine salesman. That sounds obscene,
he thought, looking down at her crotch where her slacks were pulled
tight into her vulva. God, oh God, oh God. He lit another cigarette,
and they rolled onto the main drag.

The supermarket looked like any other supermarket he had ever
been in, except that all he could get toward the spaghetti dinner was
chopped meat. The store carried no garlic, no Italian sausage, no
Italian tomatoes, no tomato paste, no oregano . . . as he looked for
these things he found himself asking the manager about each item,
and what completely angered him was the fact that the manager
looked at him as if he were some sort of strange freak, some Martian.
When he finally said, look, doesn't anybody ever make spaghetti
here, the manager said, look, boy, that ain't fewed. They bought
American ingredients and hot, sagey sausage, and he asked her, as
they left, about wine, and she told him they'd have to go over the
river where the bootleg joints were, since Jackson was in a dry
county. With that remark, he lost even his simmering lust for her—
but only temporarily. Will your old man take us over? he asked, and
she said, sure. The sun hurt their eyes, Southern style, as they
headed into the parking lot.

That afternoon, he, the driver, and the host, plus a next-door
neighbor (come over to tell the Yankees about the wonders of the
South as against the ugliness of New York) went across the river to
the bootleg town to buy wine and liquor. The cracker, who was, the
husband supposed, a "liberal" by Jackson standards, since he had a
Yankee friend and listened to Dave Brubeck, spoke tirelessly about

the fantastic stock that the bootleg joints carried. Yew don't hev nothin lahk this in New Yoke, he said, wait'll y'all see these ole boys' stock. Wheeeooo!

The ole boys' stock consisted of perhaps a hundred or two bottles of rye and bourbon, fifty bottles of gin, and some wine, domestic California, in fifths, half gallons, and gallons. The husband thought that the cracker must be joking, and as he turned to acknowledge the joke, saw him smile in triumph, and say, well, what yew boys think o' that? He smiled back and looked impressed, after all, when in Rome . . . They bought a fifth of bourbon and a gallon of red wine and on the way back stopped off at the cracker's house to meet his wife, a scrawny, somewhat pretty woman who looked at least ten years older than her husband. Their two children were playing in the yard, guffawing and drawling, and as they walked into the house the boy smashed the girl in the face with a clod of dirt, and the woman said, shoot, Luther! I'm not gonna tell you again. In the house, the cracker put on a Gerry Mulligan record and spoke of it as if the white South had invented jazz, while they had drinks and a tasteless dip with potato chips. They left as soon as they were able to do so civilly, and drove back to the friend's house in silence. It was obvious that the friend was embarrassed in front of the driver and to relieve this spoke of his wild occasional weekends in New Orleans, when he heard the driver say that that's where they were headed for next. What a town, the friend said, wow! The husband winced as he compared it to New York, how boring it all was, what is it with these people, he thought. If they can't stand New York, why do they talk about it so? He looked at a Jackson paper in the car, reading a front-page editorial about Negro hordes ruining property values in New York, and placed the paper on the car seat carefully; the whole thing was beginning to turn into a dream, it was totally unbelievable that this should happen to him. As soon as they parked the car in the drive, he walked into the house and started the spaghetti. Then he sat down and began to drink boilermakers. The afternoon passed in a haze of Dave Brubeck and Joan Baez, and he argued vehemently with both the driver and the host about the merits of the Pennsylvania countryside versus the merits of the Mississippi countryside, neither of which he cared anything about. But it was something to do, anything was better than lusting for his wife and his hostess alternately and together. The meal was finally served after the children were in bed, and the sauce that he had manufactured out of the dull ingredients was, as he knew it would be, terrible. Everybody said it was great.

Later they went across the river and got another fifth of bourbon and he got drunk enough to dance with the hostess, while the host danced with his wife. The driver sat there, telling adventure stories about hitchhiking in Europe, and smiling paternally. It was a totally dull evening, saved only by the booze. The salient fact is that they all knew this. The cracker came over later and told them about the good ole days in Jackson, when they had fights every night in the bars that used to be across the river. Then he went on to indict street gangs in New York, that's what happens when yew mix up whites and nigras, and the husband belched. Everyone laughed, and he wondered why since he hadn't realized that he'd belched. Then he fell asleep, and their last night in Jackson came to a quiet close.

Brooklyn, New York

What was horrible about the meeting after C got out of the asylum was that the husband was not really embarrassed, nor did he feel guilty. He, however, acted well, so that C might think that he felt these things. C, too, felt all right, but had to accept his own role subtly, as if he himself believed in the veridicality of the performance—which is what had kept them, underneath it all, friends, even after the months spent by C in the hospital. They always accepted each other's lies as if they were truth, but, most important, they knew of each other's acceptance. It was as if they had agreed to lie to each other in order to maintain their relationship. He thought, what she and I do all the time.

They went together to the Met to hear *Wozzeck* and spoke of it

later over drinks, until slowly the conversation turned toward the
past and the days between C's discovery of his wife's acts at P's party,
and his attempted suicide. That was some note you sent me, baby,
the husband said. When you get this I'll be dead and you killed me. I
almost went through the floor, Jesus Christ! I'm hip, C said. I kept a
carbon of it. There was silence for a moment and then they looked at
each other and C laughed, then he laughed. You son of a bitch, he
said, you goddamn son of a bitch! What are you gonna do, kid, he
said. They had another drink, and C told him how happy he was that
his wife and P had finally decided to make it together, because he was
good for the kids, and the husband agreed. So they lied warmly to
each other and their friendship resumed where insanity and despair
had cut it off.

Louisiana

This is more like it, he thought, this Spanish moss and the incredible lushness, heaviness, the perfume of this place! They drove on
through country that became progressively richer, water seemed
everywhere, or at least the feeling of the proximity of water. He had
never seen such deep green, such full-leaved trees and foliage.
Strangely, the interlude in Jackson, combined with this purposive
direction toward New Orleans, moved him toward a feeling almost
of joy: he felt toward the driver as he had felt years before, when he
first met him, felt as if he were, indeed, a friend. None of the nagging
doubts as to the worth of the trip remained with him, now, at this
moment, this part of the drive. New Orleans seemed to him a haven,
a place that beckoned him with life, not a feeling of utter futility,
questioning, as to his real motives concerning the vacation in Mexico. He didn't even feel, as he had, for so many weeks now, that they
should go directly to Mexico, without the trip to the Coast first. It
was the lack of—what?—the lack, perhaps, of a feeling of "South"
that Louisiana had. It was like a foreign land in itself, he had never
experienced it. The other Southern states he had been in had sur-

passed his expectations as far as grimness and poverty were concerned, as far as a buried violence was concerned. This state seemed
to be from some region that he had never allowed his mind to enter-
tain. So he sat, happy, thinking foolishly that the landscape had
changed not only his life, his past actions, but that it had changed the
lives and past actions of both his wife and the driver. What he also
assumed was that the future journey would be a constant spiral upward, upward, until, in Mexico, they would all find themselves perfectly happy, perfectly reconciled. After all, he thought, there is
nothing that isn't salvageable, at least in part. And how he wanted to
salvage his life. He didn't know that the excitement and pleasure of
traveling through this state, this somewhat mystical reference he
now fully committed himself to, was simply one act laid upon a series
of other acts, and that it, too, would take its part in his ultimate
psychic dismembering. For now, everything was brilliant, beautiful, the feeling of despair he had had on the first leg of the trip seemed
imaginary. This was true, this Louisiana, this country of gentleness,
warmth, the past was the past, and let it go! And, too, the very fact
they had chosen New Orleans arbitrarily, not because of necessity,
nor because of "friends to see," augured well—didn't it? The first
place they were to go for their own pleasure. Even his wife would
change, this air would warm her, her resistance would dissolve, she
would love him, love him!

Crossing Lake Pontchartrain: 25 miles, could it be true?—25
miles across a bridge, dead out over the waters, farther, farther, looking back, as the car moved at 60 mph, the land behind them receding,
farther, until, finally, nothing at all but a blur of greenish blue, a
smear, then, of no color at all, and then, nothing. The center of the
lake, horizonless. He thought of an exciting daydream he had had as
a child—to build a bridge across the ocean, to be able to drive, or
walk, to Europe—this bridge was almost it, he treasured his rich
feeling, and wanted to stop here, but felt, fearfully, embarrassed,
ashamed. They drove on, the waters calm; he wondered how it
would be to drive across in a storm, rain, pounding waves, alone in
the middle of the ocean! Ahead he saw the smoke, then the smudgy

outlines of the city, New Orleans, huddled against the shores of this fantastic lake, this bridge shooting over it. They moved closer—at five miles, the smudges resolved themselves into buildings and they drove into a gentle, drizzling rain.

Brooklyn, New York

He was so drunk that he thought the top of her garter belt was a girdle and he was struggling to pull it down, when she said, no, no, it's all right, and he looked down at her spread thighs and the dark swatch between them. Somewhere to their right he heard W and his girl laughing and the clink of a bottle against pebbles. He pushed himself into her, deliriously happy, the first time! The first time after all these months of courting. He came instantly, and forever after she thought of him as a bad lay. He lay back on the cool grass, the wind from the bay cold against his wet genitals; he watched her pull up her panties and adjust her skirt and he loved her, felt that since he had seen her do this thing in front of him, she was his, completely his. He lit a cigarette and wondered how W was making out with his girl, a girl he detested for her simpering pretensions to intelligence. Not like *his* girl. They loved each other. Hadn't she pulled up her panties in front of him? Hadn't she smiled? What was love if not that?

New Orleans, Louisiana

They decided to look for rooms in the Old Quarter, the drive through "downtown" New Orleans considerably depressing them, blunting the edge of excitement they had all felt upon approaching the city. Turning off Canal Street, down Royale, was like entering another city, one that had nothing to do with the bustling, modern nonentity they had just moved through. Somehow, by some miracle, the Old Quarter had retained its quiet beauty even though it was almost completely commercialized, ravaged by tourist traps, strip joints, and the like. The old beauty, the intimacy of the place was of such solid stock that nothing, it seemed, could harm it. All the places built to fleece the transients seemed to become one with the essential character of the Quarter, and the places changed. They were charmed, even the children looked out the windows with awe at the old houses, the grillwork, the narrow streets filled with people who walked leisurely in the light drizzle. They stopped at the curb and ordered hot dogs from a vendor, delicious hot dogs with chili and raw chopped onions, and asked him if he knew of any place where they might get rooms for a three- or four-day stay, and he told them that they were a block away from a place, small rooms, but clean and cheap, with a clean bathroom, including shower.

They got to the address, a building on the corner of Royale, and looked warily at it—it was grim, grey, a simple three-story cube of an affair, with the ubiquitous grillwork terraces running around the second and third floors—which is what decided them. They knocked at the door and it was opened by an old woman who haggled with them, until finally they reached agreement on the cost of two rooms on the same floor, with one bath to be shared. It was then that they were amazed, as they walked into the house off the street. The short alley led into a patio with bushes, flowers, and palms from which a stone stairway led to the second floor. Each room led onto a balcony, which ran completely around the hollow center of the building. It was cool and damp, but incredibly pleasant inside. The rooms were all right. The driver's was small and opened only on the balcony, but theirs was large enough to sleep them and the two children comfortably, and long shutter windows looked onto the terrace which overhung the street, teeming below. It was a fine room, and he was delighted. He looked at his wife with a love he had not felt for her in years—a love and a hope for the both of them. The children played quietly on the terrace while they unpacked their clothes, removed from the driver, unpacking in his small room, across the house from them. The rich, warm air thrilled the husband, and he took a chair out to the terrace and watched the night come on, the rain falling away to nothing as he sat and smoked, his eyes at rest on

the house across the street from which there came the sound of someone playing a piano, and well. A beautiful city, a beautiful city. He
wasn't such a fool after all, his lovely wife, his lovely children, they
loved him. He was taking them to Mexico, where they would all be
happy. And the driver. A good guy, he thought. What weird ideas
I've had of him. He was ashamed that he had remembered F's ad-
monitions concerning "backless" men. Goddamn F! As if he's such
a noble soul—drunken bastard! So he smoked on, and gazed at the
house across the street, mistaking the peace that this old city gave
him with a peace that he could only have made solid through his own
manufacture, his own mind. But it was respite; even the wagon,
parked below, seemed to him "noble," a trusted veteran: that green
lemon he would soon lose forever.

Brooklyn, New York

They were standing in the sun, the husband, W, the wives, and the
child. The child wasn't W's, he had married this lisping ass of a
woman out of pity over the fact that she had been made pregnant by
one of the neighborhood imbeciles. He looked at W, and suddenly
saw him with perfect clarity—as if he was seeing straight down past
the bones and flesh; it was, for a moment, frightening. His wife stood
before the three of them to take a snapshot.

What is he doing here with this woman? Scrawny bitch. The kid
not his, look at him, younger than I am and his face is broken with it,
is it? he thought, and shifted his angle—maybe it's the sun? No, it's
the same, it's his face that *is* broken, the sun just so bright it brings it
out clearly. I never noticed it before today.

The little boy's mouth hung open and he drooled over his new
Easter outfit, until finally his mother slapped him on the rump. Stop
drooling! W looks at her (his face broken with misery, resignation).

His wife has the camera ready, and says, ready? Stand still.

They stand, the three of them. The kid is picking his nose. W
looks down and away toward the bay, the sun making his hair look

soft and wispy, but his face, his face, he thinks. Dead. The whole stupidity of marriage to this fool. He is secretly pleased that his wife is so lovely, so perfect, their child just beginning to swell her belly will not be a drooling brat like this one.

Tell stupid to stand still, W says. W! she says, he is *not* stupid! You can be so—uncultured, sometimes. They stand still again, W looks at the camera, his wife smiles, stupidly, the child drools. Uncultured, he thinks. Her old lady thought the bathtub was a dirty-clothes hamper. Shanty Irish bastards! His anger shakes him, and he lights a cigarette. Trapped . . . not like him. W looks down at the child and his face cracks into what seems to be the preface to a howl of surrender or ennui, but he merely says, the words knifing through the calm April air, goddammit, stupid, stand still! The child looks up at him and smiles, drooling, and he looks away, mocks the child's smile. There is no movement but the wheeling gulls far off over the bay.

His wife snaps the photo, and W's wife says, how many more? How about one of you two paterfamiliars together. He walks over to W. Come on, kid, one more and we'll go have a few and let the ladies walk on home ahead of us, O.K.? Sounds—devastating, he says.

They both begin to laugh conspiratorially and W's wife's voice drones in the background, ready? Ready? Are you two paters properly stanced? W looks at him, then at his wife, yes, dear, he says, we is stanced.

They put their arms around each other's shoulders and gaze grinningly at the camera. They love each other, love even more the memory of each other. The camera snaps and W's wife says to his wife, all right, dear, let the boys go have their man-talk.

New Orleans, Louisiana

Their second night there, after eating in a small restaurant (delicious gumbo, ham steaks with red beans and rice, and rich coffee with chicory) they return to the rooming house and he sits on the terrace looking down on the crowded streets, enjoying his cigarette. He and his wife have agreed that he will go out with the driver for a few hours, then return, whereupon she will go out with the driver. This arrangement has been made by them (although the driver does not protest as it is told him) so that the driver will not have to mind the children while both of them go out together. The husband has agreed to this rather unusual arrangement through the employment of what can only be called a perverse logic; the driver has been informed over the phone that the man who has been cashing his checks for him back in Washington has sent three or four of them ahead to San Antonio, where he knows that they will stop, at the driver's sister's house, for a few days. Hence, all the bills have been paid by the husband, for which he can expect to get no recompense at all for some time. Because of this, he feels that to ask the driver to baby-sit for them would be (in the driver's eyes) unrefusable, since the driver's position has made him liable to such acts of gratitude as this one. Because of this, and the fear that the driver will think ill of him and his intentions, misconstrue them, the husband refuses to ask him to do this favor for him and his wife.

They go out, he and the driver, leaving the wife to put the children to bed and dress. They go from one bar to another, small places with quiet lights and Uncle Tom piano players, horrible garish clubs where bored Negroes play fake Dixieland, rock'n'roll joints where they are assailed constantly by B-girls. They stop for frankfurters and then go back to the rooming house, both of them slightly high. He gives the driver a twenty-dollar bill and tells him and his wife to have a good time, then sits down to read a mystery novel, listening to the breathing of his two children in the quiet, warm room. He puts the book down after an hour and goes out on the terrace to smoke, and after a while falls asleep. He wakes abruptly with a crick in his neck and looks at his watch. It is 3:30 and they are still not back. He goes inside, undresses, and gets into bed. He lights a cigarette, then hears her heels down the hall, and puts the cigarette out quickly.

She enters the room and he groans as if waking, turns heavily in bed, hating himself all this while, but wild in his desire for her. She must need him as he needs her! She must! She can't be made of clay. Are you still awake, she says. I just woke up, he says. Did you have a good time? Yes, she says, sitting on the edge of the bed and lighting a cigarette, we went to the Absinthe House and Jean Lafitte's Bar, that lovely one with the outdoor patio in the back, I think it's Jean Lafitte's. She stands and begins to remove her clothes. I love you, he says, and reaches out to touch her thigh, but she twists away from him, and says, I had Pernod frappés, terrific, and takes her slip off. I love you, he says, come here, please? What is it? she says, what *is* it? Leave your stockings and heels on, he says, and come here. You look beautiful that way. She stands and looks at him. You know how I feel about that, she says, it's sick. You're sick for asking me. You know it makes me feel like a whore. Please, he says. Please. You're so beautiful. You make me feel like a whore, she says. I . . . won't do it, no. He looks at her, his entrails churning in excitement and disgust. Maybe you'd like it if I punched you in the fucking mouth, he says. Why don't you, if it'll make you feel any better, why don't you, she says, sitting on the edge of the bed again and peeling off her stockings. He turns viciously from her and stares through the open shutters onto the terrace. She slips into bed and touches him, tenderly, pityingly. Honey, she says. You know I don't like that. He heaves himself away from her. Christ! It's bad enough without you *touching* me! They turn their backs on each other. She feels good because she was willing to offer her cold flesh to him and he refused it; he feels good because he got up the nerve to ask her to come to him as he wanted her, like a whore, and she refused him. So they sleep, each aware of fulfilling a duty.

She sleeps peacefully beside him, her conscience assuaged, her duty performed: now it is sleeping time, so she sleeps. He thinks, a compartmentalized brain, a time for everything, a space for everything, none of her emotions bleed into her other emotions, so she has, never, a pang of guilt, a feeling for the unresolved past, a concern for the future. Each moment is faced, and lived through, and

the next moment is utterly discrete from the preceding one. So she
handles her neuroses, her cruelties, so she handles this marriage,
and he doubts whether she thinks of it as unhappy; there are unhappy moments, that is all. He stares at the wall, incredulous. Can it
be that it is only now that he knows this? What *does* he know about
her? All these years and what does he know about her? Can it be that
the trip has been the source of knowledge—*that* he cannot believe,
nothing has changed but the sky, the land. And now tonight. What a
fool to think that she would feel the excitement, the possibility in this
air as he felt it. She never even mildly protested when he suggested
that they each go out with the driver, separately. And what did he
expect, that she would stay out for an hour or two and then return to
leap upon him, tongue hanging out with lust, what does he think of
her to expect her to suddenly reverse her feelings concerning him? A
romantic, he thinks, a goddamned romantic. He knew what she
would do, from the start, stay out until all the 20 was spent, then
come in, refuse him, say he was sick, that all he ever wanted to do was
fuck, forgetting that his wants never came close to being fulfilled.
She did what he knew she would do, and he became angry at her.
Rather, his anger should have been directed toward himself. Why
don't I get out of it, now? Just forget it. Things won't be better in
Mexico, things won't be better anywhere, and I know it. He closed
his eyes and tried to relax his tense body. He thought, well, at least
I'm holding on, I'm not going to be the one, let her be the one, I won't
do it. He smiled smugly, not knowing that he thought of himself as a
martyr, a sacrifice to the great god marriage. If the marriage could
be made to last, then unhappiness was merely an annoyance. What
he never understood was that he would have scorned any other marriage that remotely resembled his own as stupid, meaningless. But
he had turned what should have been self-pity into what he thought
of as nobility, what should have been anger into what he flattered
himself was strength; and what was truly her contemptuous usage
of him metamorphosed itself in his mind into what he termed childishness. So, in a sense, his dull rounds kept pace with hers—al-

though he packed the more brilliant highlights of them together and tried to think of only them as indicative of their relationship. If we were happy once, why not again? He fell into a deep, untroubled sleep, convinced of his manly acceptance of responsibility.

Brooklyn, New York

He knew very well that she had come with C, his best friend, but he was too drunk to care—he wanted her too much to care one way or the other; if C can't take care of her, fuck him, he thought, as he slid his tongue into her mouth, her back pressed against the kitchen wall. She went into the bedroom and got her coat and C stared at them drunkenly, then turned away with a lackadaisical smile. Well, how much can he care for her, he thought. They went out into the snowy night and sat at a bar around the corner, drinking Old Fashioneds— he kept running his hands up her thighs under her dress and she looked at him lustfully. After about an hour they left and he walked her to her house. They stood in the dark cold of the porch and she masturbated him, and he asked if he could see her soon, he only had another three days' leave, but he wanted to see her. She said, call me tomorrow, and kissed him. He walked up the block not even feeling the cold, and walked into a bar where everybody met, and saw C sitting alone at the bar drinking Scotch. I'm sorry C, he said, I didn't mean to steal her away . . . it's just, it's just that . . . I don't know, we really were good with each other. C looked askance at him, and said, that's O.K., old buddy. Did she at least blow you? He angered in- stantly, and was about to punch C, then realized how ridiculous that would be, after all, what *was* she to him? She's a terrific cocksucker, he said, *everybody* will tell you that. Then he took another drink, and turned back to him. You're not pissed off at me, are you? Jesus, I'm finished with her, long ago. We just see each other once in a while—he leered—on a "friendly" basis. You don't have to be bugged; let everybody have a share, I say. Why not you? He laughed with C, and ordered a drink, in his heart thick, burning hatred for him. Six months later he was discharged; two months after that he was married to her. C was best man and afterwards they had a lovely wedding supper, the two of them plus C and his future wife.

Houston, Texas

About twenty miles past the Louisiana-Texas border his son, joined unsurely but delightedly by his daughter, begins to sing, 2-4-6-8, we don't want to integrate, and he turns in alarm to them in the back, and barks harshly to shut up. His daughter begins to cry, and his son looks bewildered. Then he calms and tells them that it's a terrible thing to say, and tries to explain to them what the chant means. They don't understand but he finally makes them understand by using examples of Negro friends of theirs and telling them that the song means that these Negro friends are not good enough to be *their* friends. He says again and again, they're wrong, bad, a terrible thing to say, and then he asks them where they heard this thing. His wife breaks in to say that the last day in New Orleans she had taken them for an hour or so to a playground in the park, while he and the driver sat in their room and had a couple of beers, and they heard little white children singing this song, waving Confederate flags, and shouting. The children were fascinated, she says, but she didn't know that they had heard the words clearly enough to remember them. All right, he says, no more, they're terrible words, a terrible thing to say. He sits back in his seat and the children sit quietly, still unhappy. So the New Orleans visit has been a total disaster. And it started—so well, he thinks. So well. That's the end of that shit about trusting feelings, he thinks, no more. A lousy fucking town, a rotten, stinking town, goddamned phony French Quarter, clip joints—all those fucking phony crackers! And to poison even his children! He turns to his wife, angrily. What the hell did you stay there for, god-dammit! What, do you think they're still babies, that you can say anything in front of them—or do you think that that's good, to get

them hard! Hard! That rotten town, phony goddamn town! But—
she says. But, nothing, he says. As soon as you heard those cracker
kids with that poison you should have left the playground, and you
should have told the kids what it was all about! Haven't you got any
feelings except for yourself? Jesus Christ, ego is ego, but Jesus
Christ! The driver sits, silently, a tenuous smile on his lips. The
husband glances at him. They're not his children, and she's not his
wife, it isn't his car, or his money. In Mexico it won't be his house.
He drives, he takes what is given him, the bastard!

After the sun goes down they drive for hours on an eight-lane
speedway, heading for Houston, where they plan to spend the night
before going through to San Antonio, too far away to make in one
hop. They reach the outskirts of Houston, the memorial to the de-
feat of Santa Anna standing white against the dark sky. The motel
that they find is run-down but cheap, and they take a cabin with three
large rooms. There is no TV, but they have plenty of cold beer, and
his wife makes sandwiches on (amazingly) French bread that they've
bought on the road—it turns out, however, to be tasteless and soggy.
The children are bathed and put to bed and they play 500 rummy for
an hour or two, then his wife goes to bed and he and the driver sit and
drink beer, talking about Mexico, and the best place to go. The west
coast is the driver's suggestion, particularly since they're going to
head down from San Francisco—besides it's warm, and the little
villages are beautiful, Mazatlán, Manzanillo, Acapulco, ah, the little
cabañas on the beach, sitting in the evening drinking highballs and
watching the surf, the mountains huge behind your back, almost
coming down to the Pacific. The husband excuses himself and goes
into the bathroom to take a shower, thinking, perhaps there is something wrong with me, demanding so much from her, am I sick, to be
thrilled so after all these years to see her in fancy underwear, stockings? It shouldn't be, maybe. It *is* whorish when she wears those
things for me, my insatiable lusts. And suppose it should happen
that I became impotent if she *didn't* . . . ? Yet, so rarely do I ask, so
rarely are we happy at all, except when it is almost a rape.

He dries and gets into bed, hears the shower turned on again by the driver. He looks across at her sleeping, and places both feet against her side and shoves with all his might, hearing her groan and then the bump of her body on the floor. He is suddenly ashamed of himself, aghast at his act, and looks at her face, surprisingly visible in the dark room. She says nothing, simply stares at him with fear and anger, and he stares back at her, silent also. At this moment he knows, and she knows, too, that they will never get to Mexico, that whatever kindness occurs between them from this moment on will be a total lie, an act. Their lives together are over. She slides back into bed and turns her back to him. They won't touch each other any more, that's for certain. Now that he knows that the rest of the trip will be simply a waiting to see who will give up, or in, first, a desperately sought peace drops on him. It is this that he was waiting for— all these years! To *know* that it's over, to feel little regret, simply peace, relaxed and beneficent peace. He closes his eyes and is almost asleep in minutes. So easy to give up, done in a moment, and we both know it. Good-by, it's all over. That's why we made the trip. To separate, with manufactured reasons that would never have proved efficacious in the stability of living, together, in one place, the stability of residence. The trip was their exit, their opportunity.

San Antonio, Texas

It was perfect, absolutely perfect. They sat next to each other, as they had the whole trip, and they both knew that it was finished, he waited that morning for her to say something, but she not only refused to accept his mean act of the night before *as* mean, she made it into something it had not been, a blatant lie—she told him, as he stared at her in disbelief (but only for a moment, then he picked right up on her story, and went along with it, even *laughing*—such liars had they become), that he had tossed and turned so in bed last night that he'd knocked her on the floor. He said, yes, I saw you standing there in amazement, you were still really asleep, and she said, yes, I just vaguely remember it. He wondered if this were true—perhaps she didn't know that he had deliberately, out of despair and futility, pushed her—perhaps she really *did* think . . . but he knew this was a ludicrous idea. They both knew, they simply lied, as they had lied for years. It was a relationship of lies, omissions, hyperbole, that fed upon its own falsehood, so that after a while they even came to believe the lies, they forgot, actually, what really *had* happened at a specific time . . . as I'll forget this, he thought. In a year's time, less, I'll really believe that I knocked her to the floor accidentally, or, if not believing that, I won't remember just what I did, or why. I'll invent an argument, something, to cover the fact. And so will she. It doesn't matter now though, he thought. We both know that the rest is just a glide, just a slow glide. A wait. And how perfect, how perfect, that they should wake to rain, a sodden useless Texas rain, San Antonio occasionally glimpsed through breaks in the murk, miles away on the tablelike land. The rain really comes along as index, to us. Not true or it would have rained for months, years. He looked forward to reaching the city, he'd always liked it as a leave town when he was in the army.

He was often amazed, almost frightened himself lately, with his thoughts about the army. He had reached such a stage of ennui in his life that he thought of the army with a kind of fondness, as a place that had been for him a haven, a good place, a happy time. Youth. He was aware that this was also a lie, but he tried desperately to think of the miserable frustration and boredom of those two years and even then, even when he recalled the exact emotions he had felt at certain utterly hopeless moments during that time, they seemed to him better than this, better, anything was better than this. He gilded that life, made it romantic. And mixed with this egregious nostalgia were his unshakable feelings of guilt concerning his children. If he had stayed in, he would not have fathered them, he would not have felt so lost, so utterly lost in his role as father. He had failed, and although the children did not know it, they would soon enough. Even now, he imagined the leave-taking that would occur on that day when they decided that the lies could no longer sustain them. He felt that perhaps he should "try again"—for the good of the children, and thought for a moment of talking to her, honestly and seriously, about it. But it was merely the thought of a moment since he knew that their life together had reached a point so ugly that nothing *should* rescue it, further, he knew that it would have been so even without the birth of the children. He backed alarmedly away from the candor of such an admission: it made even the good things bad, the possible and kind, tainted. He looked straight down the road.

San Antone was as he had remembered it, except that he didn't like it now, at all. It seemed stale, used, so dreary and grey in the rain. The Alamo still stood across the way from the Memorial to Davy Crockett, both in the center of downtown, the streets still packed with GIs and airmen, but he had no interest at all, he wanted some lunch, he wanted out of the car. They drove swiftly through the downtown area and out into the suburbs to the driver's sister's house. She was expecting them, and after the introductions, they got their gear out of the car and into the house, and the sister made sleeping arrangements. She was a heavy-set, rather homely girl who spoke quietly to her three children, who soon made friends with their children, and they all went into the back room to play. The four of them washed and sat down to lunch, and he let the driver and his wife carry the conversation: he felt stunned, beaten, there was nothing to say, so he simply ate, and drank coffee afterwards. The sister's husband came home soon after, and there were more introductions, then they fed the children and put them to bed, and then all of the adults ate while the driver and his brother-in-law talked of cars and mechanics—the brother-in-law worked in a garage. The husband was dragged into the conversation since they started to speak of the troubles they had had on the road and he swung along with them, why not? He went out then with the driver and they bought bourbon and returned and the host made highballs. Things slowly became bizarre to him, the drunker he got, since the conversation began to turn slowly toward an article on surgery that had appeared in the *Reader's Digest*; the same thing that they had talked about in the driver's home in Illinois; he sat, dumbfounded, looked at his wife, who was nodding and talking animatedly along with the others, then he chimed in, again, he thought, why not? It's all madness. He spoke of his medical experiences, his cuts, his injuries, his stitches and bruises and lacerations, real and imagined. It was incredible to him, his world was gone and he talked on and on, then suddenly he was aware that his wife was not in the room and that his daughter was crying. He got up and excused himself, went into the room where his children were. His wife leaned over the bed, patting and stroking his daughter while she cried, daddy, daddy, I want daddy. Here I am, baby, he said, here's daddy, what's the matter? Mommy and I are right here, now just you go to sleep, we're right in the next room. He stood there, next to his wife, and felt so utterly helpless, so completely inept, that he could have screamed in anguish, but he patted and stroked his daughter, then said to his wife, go on back, she'll be O.K. in a minute, go on back in. His wife turned, left, and he continued to soothe his girl, until finally she went back to sleep. He sat in the dark for a long time, looking at her face, then over at his son, thinking, failure, failure, no right to do it to them, no right at all. Then he got up and went back into the living room, smiling as he emerged into the light, saying, she's fine, sound asleep now, sitting down again, still smiling as he accepted a fresh drink, proud of his smile. Not even she knows how I feel, he thought. I can fool even her. He thought of this as triumph.

Brooklyn, New York

The woman in the casket, in lavender silk, her cheeks pink and bloated, her hands folded over a rosary and missal, was someone, for sure, someone, but not his mother. He kneeled, surrounded by relatives, kneeling also, people whom he had not seen in years, they listened to the young priest pray, joined with him in response. His wife stood at the back, stood! As if she *is* a Protestant, goddamned bitch, a good Protestant, can't she do this for me, just this? What can it possibly mean to her, to kneel, yet she stands, all such a bore, she is concerned because her mother has to mind the children, a great inconvenience that his mother has died, that's what it comes to, simply an annoyance, and nothing more. He had a fantasy of standing, walking across the heavy rug of the sweet-smelling funeral parlor and smashing her in the face, down!! you bitch, get down before death, at least, get down! But he kneeled and followed the priest's voice, looked up at the casket, his mother's face in profile, the tortured face calmed by the dubious skill of people whose names he had never heard, whose faces he had never seen. And the owner of the funeral parlor a fag, he remembered him as a young man, when he was only a boy, mincing about the streets, drinking in the neighborhood bars, he repelled him. Now the husband spoke to him pleasantly, that is becoming an adult? The priest was leaving, and everybody rose, he went to the priest and thanked him, walked to his wife. Why don't you go out and get some coffee for yourself, he said. We've got another three hours here, you know. I know it's just too much for your delicate sensibilities, but people only die once, you don't have to worry about it, she won't die any more. She opened her mouth to speak to him, but he said, forget it, let's not talk about it any more at all, it's too much, it's all over, tomorrow she'll be buried, and that's that. She turned, and, smiling at some of his relatives, walked down the stairs to the street. He sat in a straight chair, his hands folded, and tried to feel something for this corpse, but it wasn't his mother, his mother was gone, her life had been a daily loss of strength, of courage, at the end she had been cheated out of everything. What could he expect of his own feelings, that they would be warm and full? He felt completely hollow, and missed his father as he had never missed him before, missed him and hated him, since he had not come, nor had he sent flowers, not even a card. Dirty bastard, dirty son of a bitch bastard! He thought that he would cry, but instead, walked over to the casket: then he cried, but not for her, cried bitterly and silently for himself, his hash of a life, the hash of all their lives, while his relatives kept a respectable distance from him and his grief, his loss. How cheap he felt, how cheap and dishonest. But nothing could stop him from crying, and he stood, looking down at that pink face, the candlelight glittering off the diamonds of the engagement and wedding rings on the stranger's hand. The smell of flowers was making him nauseous and he accepted the nausea gladly, as penance.

San Antonio, Texas

The next night, the driver's sister and her husband served as baby-sitters, and the three of them left after they were assured that the children, and especially the girl, were all right. Her outburst and nervousness of the night before was something unexpected, it was the first time so far that she had seemed thoroughly depressed and exasperated by the trip. But the day had been a good one for them, they had played in the little backyard playground that was set up there, and eaten hamburgers with soda outdoors, and they seemed content. So this opportunity to go out was seized by the three of them.

They were going to the house of one of the driver's old college friends, a man who now ran a wholesale drug business, and who made large amounts of money out of this racket. He lived in a phony "Southern" house in one of the better sections of town, complete with white pillars, driveway, and huge lawn. They walked up the path after parking the car and went in to meet him. He was there with two other friends, one, a rather short and fat man, who sat intent on smiling, the other a tall, dark man, the host's co-renter, attired somewhat fantastically in a blue silk dressing gown and white ascot. The host was tall and red-faced and looked like a defensive back. The three of them greeted the arrivals, and the host immediately mixed a batch of Martinis. The three young men were intent on being amusing, and the husband took them all in with a glance and put them down as San Antonio hipsters. He felt shabby in his levis and desert boots, and sat in a chair as unobtrusively as possible to wait patiently for his Martini. The dressing-gowned one put on a Frank Sinatra record and asked his wife to dance, and they did so, while the talk began to warm up a bit around the room. He felt better when it seemed that they all envied him his "free" existence, this trip, the money that they knew he must have in order to do all this; he was also quite pleased that they ogled his wife, and took turns dancing with her. He sat, and talked of New York and jazz, and all the things he was sure they knew nothing of, selecting his tales in such a way as to make himself seem an intimate of all those things which are sug- gested by the phrase "night life." Nor did he know that it was all ludicrous, that they thought him, finally, ludicrous, slugging down his Martinis now, realizing that they were putting him on, and help- less to do anything about it. His wife was having a fine time, as long as she can dance, she has a fine time, he thought. What a fucking outlook on life. The driver was in the middle of old college tales now, and they laughed, crowding each other's narratives along, so that each could contribute. He sat, stupid, dumb, he felt more com- pletely out of place here than he had felt back at the sister's house, and finally he got up to dance with his wife. After the first few steps he tried to do a fancy dip, lost his balance, and fell, hearing every- body's laughter, hating the fat man who helped him to his feet, hat- ing the voice of Frank Sinatra as it leaped into the air of the room, his fingersnapping, all a bunch of squares! A bunch of fucking squares, all of you, he thought. Then he slumped into a chair and fell asleep.

An hour or so later, they woke him, saying they were going over to a joint called La Paloma, on the west side, the Mex side of town, for *cabrito* and chili. He got up and went out with them, and they drove over in the dressing gown's Pontiac, his wife laughing at something, while his head pounded. Inside, they gave some money to some shabby *mariachis* who were hanging around, and they were sere- naded while they ate. The host told his wife that *cabrito* was baby goat, and she made a face, but bravely ate it, while these habitués chuckled as they stoked away what seemed to him huge quantities of food. He ate a little chili and some refried beans, got up, walked out to the street, and puked. He came back inside, stupidly thinking that they had not known why he had gone outside and listened then to jokes about him not being able to hold down the Mex food, Texas whisky, and all the rest of it. The last half hour or so was spent in a serious discussion of the virtues of living in a town like San Antonio, how it was small enough to be slow and quiet, but really hip, if you knew the places, and the right people.

They drove back to the host's house and there the three of them transferred to their Ford. The husband insisted on driving, but the driver said, you're pretty under the weather, buddy, you think you should? He said, goddammit, it's my fucking car, and got behind the wheel. Halfway home he scraped the fenders against a curbing on the highway, and stopped the car, got out, and puked again. You're right, he told the driver, and got into his usual place. When they got in the house, his wife and the driver sat in the dark living room for a nightcap, but he went to bed immediately, falling into a drunken coma-like sleep.

Lawton, Oklahoma

Halfway there, he thought. Just through the West now, and then a couple of weeks in San Francisco, and then down to Mexico; he forced himself to complete this itinerary in his mind. Northern Texas had pleased him, he saw the beginnings of Western topography there, the land flattening out, getting dryer, less populated, and here and there in the distance, a mesa, purplish in the dust haze over everything. Now they were between Wichita Falls and Lawton, and the night had come. His old army friend, and the driver's old college friend as well, J, lived in Lawton now, helping his older brother out as a bartender and emcee at a little clip-joint night club, designed to separate the Fort Sill GIs from their monthly pay. He was so anxious to see J, it had been three years since he had last been in New York, and he had written occasionally, asking them all to come out sometime to see him, so now, they were (unbelievably) in Oklahoma and on their way to say hello, stay a few days. They knew that J was living with a divorcee in the town, the daughter of one of the more prosperous merchants, and that he was having a lot of trouble with the police, since he was a Mexican and the girl was what they call in the West an anglo. J had romanticized himself almost out of existence in every situation of his life, and in this one had painted himself as a pariah in the town, constantly harassed by the police as a troublemaker, a local hood. The husband as well as his wife and the driver knew J's proclivity for lying, and so took all these stories with a smile, and put up with his elaborations and hyperbole in return for the good humor he usually showed, for his complete, though studied, casualness in life. The husband was not prepared to meet a woman that J had said was beautiful, he simply expected to meet another woman. But she *was* beautiful, scrubbed, tanned, tall, with long, beautiful legs and high, firm breasts, a handsome, open face, and honey-colored hair. He hated J the moment he saw her, hated his wife even more an hour later, and later in the evening, hated the driver more than both of them because of his sleeplessness, his prying watchfulness. Who the hell did he think he was? My fucking wife doesn't love me anyway, he thought, so who cares?

They parked the car in front of the little night club and the husband got out and walked downstairs, eager now to see J, laugh again with him. He saw a man in the hat-check room, a replica of J, although he was older and heavier, and he knew that it was J's older brother, and he walked to him, and spoke. There were the usual greetings, and then J walked out of the club itself, dressed in a dark-blue suit, a black shirt, and a black tie. You son of a bitch, he said. You son of a bitch! Where is everybody? They went upstairs quickly, and he laughed when he saw the driver and the wife in the car, the children sleepy in the back. Come on, come on, he said, we'll go out to my girl's house, I'll take the rest of the night off. You can all sleep there tonight and tomorrow I'll get you a nice cabin at a motel I know. The guy is a good friend of mine, so he'll put me on the cuff—I'll pay, you're my guests . . . Goddamn! How are you all, what's new, how was the trip? They got into the car and drove to the edge of town to a small wooden house, and parked in the driveway. As the driver turned off the ignition, the lights in the living room went on, and then the door opened and a girl stood in the light flooding out onto the path. That's my baby, J said. They got out of the car, the husband carrying his son, the wife the daughter, and walked to the house. My friends, J said, and introduced everybody. The girl was beautiful and the husband looked at her carefully. Later, after the children were asleep in the bedroom, and they were working on a quart of Scotch, he felt that he was falling in love with her, she was kind and lovely, she was beautiful, she smiled so warmly at him. He kept looking over at his wife, and each time he scrutinized her face she seemed more gross, worn, older. He hated J for having this woman, for having this freedom, and he hated all of them for being here, in this room with them. She had come to the door in a robe and pajamas, but had changed to a red sweater and tight slacks, and he ogled her, helpless before this feeling which swamped him. J was playing his usual memorized bits from *Rhapsody in Blue* and they were all relaxing with the whisky, talking, telling of their trip, their breakdowns, as if they had been jokes. Later, when they put on records, he made it a point to dance twice with his wife, so that when he asked J's girl to dance it wouldn't seem obvious. He didn't realize that his wife didn't care, at this point he was so obsessed with holding J's girl in his arms that he thought his desires must be clear to them all. As he asked her to dance, J asked his wife to dance, and the driver sat, smiling and talking with them as they moved around the large, smooth wooden floor. It was fantastic to hold her, and he danced beautifully, he thought he danced beautifully, at any rate, although it was simply that she followed him so well that dancing was easy for him.

He got drunker, to that point, in fact, that the time seemed to slip away so fast that he thought only an hour had passed when actually it had been two. J had set up cots for them in the room and J, drunk too, lay down and was instantly asleep. The driver sat on his cot smoking and talking with his wife, who had also lain down to sleep.

He kept dancing, pushing his groin against the girl, feeling her respond, slyly feeling the sides of her breasts. He stayed at the far end of the room with her, where it was darker, and he was aware that he was foolishly hoping that no one noticed his actions. Suddenly he realized that the record was over, and grinning callowly, he walked over to the phonograph, holding her hand, and put it on again. Again? she said, but not with annoyance. It was at that moment that he knew, simultaneously, that his wife was asleep, the driver was still sitting on his cot watching them, and he could have her if he could get her alone.

His mind was a storm of plans and schemes, all foolish. He wondered if he could fuck her right on the floor, damn the driver. Then he realized that he couldn't, he didn't know exactly why, but he knew that he couldn't. Should he ask her to take a walk? To go out on the lawn with him? He looked out of the corner of his eye and the driver was lying down now, but still awake, still watching. Is he my wife's watchdog? He was furious. The record ended again, and he said that he needed a drink. So do I, she said. She sat and he made two stiff, tall Scotches with plenty of ice but no water, and they sat facing each other, talking about her ex-husband, and about J, and the troubles that they had had together. She was terribly drunk, he realized, and sitting in the chair with her legs apart, her back arched so that her breasts filled the sweater tightly. Oh God, help me, help me. I love this woman!

He couldn't figure out what happened then, but she had just told him something about J, when J leaped out of the cot and rushed across to her, smashed her across the face with the back of his hand, screaming at her and trying to hit her again. The husband was out of his chair in an instant, stumbling, but getting across the space that separated them quickly. The driver beat him though and pulled J away, slammed him against the wall, screaming as loud, and telling him that if he did that once more, he'd beat the piss out of him. J went utterly limp, and began to cry. He walked out of the room and into the bathroom and she followed him. From behind the closed door he heard sounds of argument, then weeping, then her voice, soothing, quieting. Then there was silence and he knew that they were making love. He looked, ashamed, at the driver, who had got into bed again, took off his clothes and got into his cot. His wife, next to him, slept on. The next morning their hangovers were vicious, everyone sat dazedly at the table in the breakfast nook and talked as if the night before had not occurred. He shoveled his fried eggs into his mouth dutifully; he loathed everyone, including himself. What he needed was a drink, and there was nothing to drink but some flat club soda. The children played on the front lawn, in the bright sunlight, while they sat over a second pot of coffee and cigarettes, telling old jokes.

Later, J offered to take them over to the motel he had mentioned the night before, but the husband was so disgruntled by the turn things had taken that he suggested they leave a day earlier than originally planned. His wife and the driver seemed relieved that he had suggested this, and quickly agreed, saying that they wanted to get to Santa Fe a couple of days before Thanksgiving, which they had planned on spending with some old friends from New York: they didn't want to arrive so late that the wife wouldn't have time to help with shopping and cooking. J protested, saying that he had planned a picnic for the next day, and besides, it was only about ten hours from Lawton to Santa Fe. The thought of a picnic was appalling to the husband, all of them out in the woods somewhere with his stupid desire for this girl growing with each moment, J's anger with her boiling just beneath the surface, and the offal of his own relationship with his wife made more fetid by the potency of these tensions, these angers. He refused, they really wanted to leave, it would give them a good jump if they left today. His wife and the driver nodded agreement, and they finally decided it would be best. J seemed genuinely sorry. As the car moved out of the driveway, the canvas carryall strapped down carefully, the children amid their baskets and boxes of toys and books, they waved at him and her, both of them standing in the doorway, waving back, J's arm around her waist gingerly. He seems so sad, the husband said, so sad and bugged. The car swung from the street onto the road which joined with the highway, the sun was bright. They figured on making Santa Fe by 9 or 10 that night.

Brooklyn, New York

He opened the door of their basement apartment and there he was, J. He wore a black raincoat and a cigarette dangled from his mouth, his heavy horn-rimmed glasses gave him the look of someone masquerading as an Indian at a party. J! J! Holy Jesus! It's been years! And it had. He hadn't seen him since 1953, and now it was 1957. Thought I'd drop in and see you, J said. He stepped inside and put his bag on the floor, it was small, the brown leather scarred and stained. His wife came into the living room and looked at both of them. You know about J, he said. I've told you all about him. Oh, of course, she said. What a surprise. J took off his coat and opened the bag, pulled out a quart of tequila. Some of the old juice, he said, smiling. His son came in from the yard to get his gun and holster, and stopped short when he saw J. This is my boy, the husband said. J turned and scooped him up. What a big fella, he said. How are you, buddy? The husband was opening the bottle and asking his wife if they had lemons.

That was the beginning of the ride downhill, for J's stay lasted four months, during which time, in a simple exchange for his wit and jokes, he ate his old friend's food, drank his whisky, invaded his privacy, borrowed his money, stole another friend's money from his overcoat, snorted with contempt at the husband's steady employment, read imitations of Hemingway that he had written in college, and tried to rape C's wife while he was in the hospital. The husband went faithfully to work each morning. When he finally asked him to leave, J cashed a check for bus fare in a delicatessen that the husband frequented in the neighborhood. It bounced and he had to make it up out of his 75-dollar-a-week salary. His wife told him how relieved she was that J was finally gone. Getting in my way all day long, is what she said. The husband worked on, deeper than ever stuck in the morass of being a nice guy: oh yes, he was tops. And it was really great to have the driver as a friend. They sat together many nights and talked about J, about what a prick he was, but . . . but, for some reason, you always had to forgive him, no matter what he did. The driver forgave him. You just had to forgive a guy like that, a real drifter, an adventurer who didn't give a damn about anything. Including people, or, more exactly, especially people, the husband offered, and they both laughed indulgently and with sublime generosity.

New Mexico

The land was a throwback to some time when monsters walked and crawled the earth. Great vistas of reddish soil, preposterous mesas blue, purple, black in the distance. His heart shriveled at the beauty, the space, the utter barrenness of the country; no men belonged here, they were simply allowed to stay by the land's good graces, they squatted here, battling the climate, the sand, the sterility constantly. The highway stretched, flat and boring, into the distance, meeting the horizon at some point which was a seeming dream—or nightmare. Ahead of them lay huge ranges of mountains, snow-peaked, brilliant and remote, intransigent; no vegetation was visible to the eye, nothing grew there, winds swirled and tortured the powdery snow. They were entering the country that was most fitting for them all; he stared, awed by the silence, the incredible brightness of the sun, the clarity of the air; it was getting difficult to breathe.

Perhaps the driver, he thought. Perhaps, somehow, he will feel the contempt, the apathy, between us and somehow enter, somehow "force" himself into the middle. But *him* as a father for these children: if he is a backless man, he must also be a man without balls. To so grovel, accept what I deign to give, accept whatever I decide he may eat for supper, what he may drink in the evening, accept even where it is we should sleep. He has no say, although he has been spending his money, since San Antonio, on gas and oil at least. Let him, it's his car, this goddamned thing is his; we are passengers. A complete passivity, sleeps where he falls—if she should make a movement toward him, he would accept that also, he would call it love. And the children like him, no? He plays with them, he is more a father to them than I am. And it would take nothing for her to leave me, she has to do it, that's what this trip is all about. Oh my God, to so lie, to so delude ourselves that it is to salvage our marriage. Salvage a mountain of slush, better. He solidly faced for the first time, without equivocation, the truth of all of it; it was a desperate attempt at aggravation, to rub to the point of unbearable agony an already painful sore. And someone will quit, and this mustachioed and epicene creature will salve her with a sexual balm; and, yes, call it love.

San Francisco, California

The third day after they had left him he decided he had to talk to J, and so called him one night, long distance to Lawton. He wasn't at the club but his brother said that he might get hold of him at his girl's house . . . this was his night off. He called, and she came to the phone. Her voice was cool and aloof, and he imagined her face to the mouthpiece of the phone: still beautiful, of course, but what had he really wanted with her? He didn't really want her, did he? Besides, J, he would never do that to J, his old friend. J? she said. Yes, he's here, I'll call him for you. There was a space of about a minute, then he heard J's voice, what is it, man? What's up? How's San Francisco, you having a good time there? J, he said, listen, I had to talk to you, I don't want to bug you, but I had to talk to you. They left, together, they just left, she says she's in love with him, in *love* with him! Holy shit! What, he said. Who—who left, they *left*? Who's in love? When did all this happen? He told him, how, when, how she had told him one night and the next day they had gone. I let them take the car, the kids are with them, they said they're going to San Antone, he can get

a job there with his friend, the guy who has the drug place. Jesus
Christ! J said, well, what *the* hell about that? They gonna stop here
in Lawton, did they say? Yes, he said, he said they'd stop there to talk
to you before going down to San Antone. Yeah, he said, I know why,
they want me to approve, show the world, ho ho, that they have
nothing to be ashamed of. It's love! J, he said, J, what am I going to
do about it? Hell, man, I'll tell you what to do. You get a goddamn
plane and get your ass over here to Lawton and shoot them both, just
shoot them. How the fuck he could do that to you I don't know, the
son of a bitch. How he could *do* that to you. J, he said, I can't do that,
don't you think I thought of it? I can't do that. Well, man, he said,
that's the only solution I can think of, just do them in, goddamn
women! They spoke for another five minutes or so, then hung up.

The husband stood for a moment, his hand still on the phone,
controlling the nausea that was threading through him. J's voice had
filled him with loathing and horror.

Santa Fe, New Mexico

The people that they were going to see were old friends from New
York who had gone out to New Mexico to get away from the almost
ghostly presence, in New York, of the woman's ex-husband. The ex-
husband had been deceived for years by these two and felt, after he
and his wife were finally divorced, that he had the right to visit and
eat dinner with the new couple whenever he wanted; that he owned
a portion of their lives. So they had left to get out of the very air of
the city, and had come here to Santa Fe, which they secretly, individ-
ually, loathed. Neither would mention this fact to the other. At this
time, as the car approached Santa Fe, they had been given an offer of
a house, rent free, to live in as caretakers of a sort, in Taos, up in the
mountains, and they were thrilled at the idea. They would soon
speak to their guests openly of their hatred of Santa Fe, with its
spurious attempts at remaining "pristine," its hopelessly shabby
aura of "history" which the town fathers did their best to promul-

gate. But Taos was really up in the mountains, the houses separated from each other by miles, and the children would have plenty of room to play and run. The children were of the wife's union with her first husband, and while the younger son liked his stepfather, the older hated him, thought of him as an interloper, and spoke to him with contempt and nastiness, which the mother defended. She would rather argue bitterly with her husband than reprimand her son. Into this family came her husband's daughter, by his first marriage, shipped by plane to New Mexico by her grandmother, with a telegram the day before as sole warning. This girl had lived with her mother—a drug addict—and a series of junkie "lovers" for three or four years, most of which had been spent in orphanages and homes. The grandmother sent her on the pretext of wanting to give her back to her father, who was now, as she said, "settled in," but she actually was terrified at the idea of giving her granddaughter a home herself. So these two adults and three children made a kind of "family" in Santa Fe, the man, M, out of work, and his wife, R, also out of work. They lived on the gratuitous and sporadic financial assistance sent them by the ex-husband. It was a grim life, some contentment and hope being injected, finally, into it by the news of the rent-free house in Taos. All this information and complaint flooded the visitors within hours of their arrival. But things seemed better now as they laughed in the blue dark and dust, shaking hands, kissing. The driver unloaded the car in silence. In two days it would be Thanksgiving.

It will be strange to see M again, he thought. I wonder if he's happy with her. Jesus, she's a hard woman, poor O went through the flames of hell married to her all those years. But M is tougher, he thought. He'll put her in her place, particularly about those kids—O let them get away with anything and they shit all over him. It'll be a time out for us too, he thought. Maybe we'll even be able to have some laughs, get off this goddamn road for a while and out of these motels. Not that there's hope, Christ, no. But maybe she'll just decide to break it up, just leave, I'll take the car, and the driver can get a fucking bus back to his sleepy and friendly lil ole town in the heartlands. Make it clean, oh, it will have to be clean, I don't care if they have anything going between them, she's not so utterly idiotic to go *away* with this creep. We might even be human here, Jesus, M and R have always been sane, anyway. He knew next to nothing of M and less of R, and less than nothing about their jointure. He came to learn that if that was sanity, it was the sanity of guerrilla warfare. But he hoped that he could spend a week or two, drunk, and laughing, and let the trip be forgotten until they got back into the car for its last leg.

The house in Santa Fe was fairly pleasant, with four rooms and a bath, and a large "backyard" which was actually a half acre or so of tangled brush and sand leading to a dry arroyo which acted as the boundary between their property and their neighbor's. M and R seemed happy, and the first night they spent there, despite the complaints that peppered their conversation, was passed pleasantly enough, with the usual old talk about the city, friends, and the like. The children were delighted to have children that they knew to play with, and the next day was as pleasant, the husband going into town with the driver and M to buy liquor and wine for the Thanksgiving dinner. The two wives had planned to go in later for the turkey and vegetables, and the husband was thoroughly aware that he was being called on to supply the money for all these things, but felt no rancor toward his old friend, rather, he pitied him that he couldn't find any work at all in the town. They had been living on cheap cuts of meat, oxtails, red beans, for months now, and were making the best of it. M told him about the move to Taos, which was to be completed by a week after Thanksgiving, and was apologetic that it should so fall out that the move coincided with their arrival. But the husband told him that they'd be delighted to help in the move, with two station wagons, instead of one, it would go that much faster, and then they could spend maybe a week at Taos with them, if that was all right. Which it was. The driver thought the whole thing was a good idea. After they bought the liquor M took them to a couple of bars in the middle of town where they spoke to some friends of M's, mostly arty and craftsy types who had moved to Santa Fe because of its beauty, its inaccessibility, its light, its climate, numbers of reasons that all seemed to be far removed from the production of arts or crafts. But they were pleasant enough, albeit a shade desperate. They all, these people of Santa Fe, had that quality of desperation about them; the husband couldn't help feeling that they were afraid of the thin air, the terrifyingly brilliant sun, the endless blue sky. There was something sinister about the neat, the charming town, with its dirt roads, its ancient square, the thick-walled Palace of the Governors, the first church ever erected in the United States, the mountains beautiful and remote that ringed the horizons. The faces were pale, faded-looking, the look that old denim gets; he wondered why nobody tanned in this strong sun, but instead, blanched. They drove home to a supper of chile and pinto beans, with plenty of cold beer and crisp crackers. It was the first time in six weeks that supper at the house had been more than a necessary ingestion of calories.

The husband was troubled, although he felt himself more relaxed than at any time since the beginning of the trip. M and R seemed to make as many references as possible to the marvel that was their sex life together—it was something hyper-human, all-consuming, extraordinary in every way. What troubled him about this was that they seemed to tacitly imply that his own sex life with his wife was miserable, as if they *knew* definitely that it was. He would have been less annoyed, perhaps, if he had known that they *did* know this fact. His wife had in R a former confidante, someone whose advice she had sought many times on the telephone. M and R looked upon him with pity. Their references to their own marriage were half-lie and half-cruelty, that too-human cruelty of displaying what one has to someone who has it not. And, too, their pity was mixed with contempt. But the husband, and his wife, joked along with them, lying as they had always lied. Neither one of them cared any more about anything affecting the other, but their familiar patterns of banter helped to foster the illusion that they did.

The other troublesome aspect to him was his feeling of guilt over his new-found affluence. It seemed almost monstrous to him that he should have money to travel, live in Mexico, do exactly what he wanted, finally, and to be here with these old friends who were just maintaining themselves from day to day. Supplying the majority of food and drink seemed little enough, he felt as if he should offer assistance in the way of actual cash; yet he dared not broach this to M, fearful that he would be hurt by the implication that he wasn't capable of supporting his family. But M seemed cheerful enough, now that they were readying for the move to the rent-free (and much larger) house in Taos, so it seemed discreet to simply let the whole thing ride . . . perhaps when they started west again, their last day, he would be able to press something on him, until that day, it was a genuine pleasure for him to be able to supply what had become to their hosts, luxury.

Hovering outside these central concerns of the husband, not quite tangible and certainly not articulate, was the mood of the driver. The husband sensed in him a growing resentment, a feeling of sheer apathy toward him, but, since it was not salient, nor anywhere near salient, he ignored it. Yet he could not help but feel that the driver was resentful, not actually of him, but more of the situation in which he found himself; that it was obvious to him that they were actually no longer married, that they were playing some sort of shabby drama out to the end, neither one of them with enough strength or honesty to terminate things. A perverse mummery of love. Further, the husband was sure that the driver knew that he was, in some unspoken way, expected to act as catalyst in this affair, expected to move in between them in some way, or, on the other hand, move *out* from between them so that their coldness toward each other could turn, thoroughly, to ice without him as their witness to embarrass them. This enforced position, into which he had been placed so subtly, set him against both of them. So the husband thought. What would he do? The husband, inarticulately, knew that he would think, this traveler, that his action, whatever it might finally be, would be thought by him to be an independent one, but he would be wrong, since he had not reckoned with a man and woman whose needs and desires were so submerged, so camouflaged, that their emergence sometimes *appeared* to be at others' bidding, but were not.

Taos, New Mexico

They came off the climbing road at its crest and moved straight into madly swirling snow. The valley stretched out far below them to the left, and ringing it, the gaunt Sangre de Cristo range loomed through the powdery snow falling in the valley. It came from no direction, but simply enveloped the car, and the rented trailer behind it, laden with household goods and a refrigerator which a friend of M's in Albuquerque had given him. They were to open the house today, move the heavier stuff in, then the next day, or the one following, the family would move. The women and children had stayed back at the house in Santa Fe, packing dishes, pots and pans, and silverware, while the men, despite a bitter, grey morning and stinging snow flurries, drove north to Taos after loading the trailer. They used the husband's Ford since M's battered Rambler couldn't possibly be trusted to haul a load up the mountain road that led into Taos. Even the Ford had trouble as they hit the snow-swept road and the wild gusts that almost obliterated the little town of Taos before them. They moved forward slowly into the grouped adobes, white smoke streaking from their chimneys. They drove on, beyond the town and down the road that led to the outlying sections, Ranchos de Taos. Here, the houses were spread out, most of them at least a quarter mile apart, and M looked at each turnoff road that they passed, trying to recognize landmarks by which he might ascertain their direction. But it all seemed no use, they turned up a few of these roads, bouncing in and out of frozen ruts, but after a mile or so the road tapered off to desert and brush, a solitary house standing at the edge of the desert stretching away to the mountains in the distance—not M's house. They decided, then, to ask someone where the right road was, and since M had already met some of the people who were living here, they went to one of the houses far out on yet another narrow road. The weather was clearing, but the air had become terribly cold, and the sky still seemed to hold tons of undumped snow, the tops of the mountains completely obscured by the heavy grey clouds.

The house they entered was a rambling adobe one, as were all the houses they had thus far seen. M's friend opened the door, comfortably dressed in corduroys and workboots, flannel shirt. His wife sat on the couch in the living room, holding a small child. A huge brick fireplace held several fat logs which burned brightly; all in all, a pleasant room. The man, after the greetings and introductions, brought a bottle of rye out from the kitchen and they drank and thawed out in front of the fire, while he gave M detailed directions. It seemed that one of the roads that they had passed again and again in their search was the right one. They had avoided it because of a hump of soil at the entrance from the main road which gave it an unused look. But that *was* the road. They finished the drinks and left, got back into the car.

They found the right road now with no difficulty at all, M's new house perched on a little hill at the end of it. It was a beautiful house, set slightly back from the road, and separated from it by a low adobe wall. The house itself was also adobe, and a building removed from it served as a garage and spare room, which could easily have been converted into a shop, or workroom, two large windows set in it and a large fireplace at one end. After investigating this outbuilding, they moved the car as close as they could to the front door of the main building, then turned so that the trailer faced the door. In the howling wind and snow of the 60-mile drive up, the ropes holding the refrigerator had turned to solid ice, and they struggled with the knots, buffeted by flat, tearing winds that came directly off the floor of the valley.

M had opened the door which led directly into the living room, then propped it back with a piñon faggot, one of a small pile which still lay in the small woodshed just outside the house. Sweating and cursing, the three of them finally opened the knots and lugged the heavy refrigerator into the house, stood for a moment, resting in the living room, grateful to be out of the cold wind. They lifted again then, carried it back through the rooms and into the kitchen, where M plugged it in to test it—but the electricity had not yet been turned on, nor had they a bottle of gas outside the kitchen for the range and the one gas heater which was built into the wall in what would, M said, be the children's room. The husband was deeply impressed by the house: it was truly beautiful, large rooms with fireplaces, picture windows that looked out on the mountain ranges surrounding, red tile floors, and beautifully carved doors separating rooms. He pulled out a pint of bourbon he had brought and they closed the door, sat on the floor, and passed the bottle. So, tomorrow, M said, and we'll be in, all I've got to do is get the gas and electric cooking, and we're set. They drank half the whisky and got up, walked outside (it was getting dark), and got back into the car.

Back in the town, M took care of the details concerning the utilities, and then suggested they go to the Taos Inn for a couple of drinks. When they got there the barroom was empty and quiet, and the warmth of the place was inviting. They sat at a table and ordered dark Mexican beer and whisky and began to talk of the new house, the possibilities now of M making it without any trouble. The husband reassured himself that M wanted them to stay for at least a week now, enjoy just sitting around without the headache of moving. They continued drinking, the driver becoming more sullen as he got drunker, until he finally refused to speak at all: the husband was delighted, vaguely aware at last that he was exerting a subtle pressure on the driver—who had to move, and soon. You have to do it, he thought, what else? You don't expect me, or her, to walk out with no real reason. He really didn't believe there was a reason that he could effectively employ. The fact of their unhappiness seemed the emptiest of motives.

They were in the car, and it was pitch black, somewhere from the border, perhaps, a Mexican station broadcast over the radio, which played loudly, so loudly that the car was a box of noise, they couldn't hear their own laughter as they passed around a bottle of rye that the husband had bought before they left Taos. The driver hunched over the wheel, his brights flooding the straight road ahead of them, the car moving shudderingly, up and down the dips and grades at 90. The husband thought, maybe we'll crash, that will be that, he'd rather crash than live with the choice he's got to make, the fucking assless wonder, he wants to crash, but what a shame to kill M. Somewhere in the husband's mind he was sorry that he would die, too, and leave her to wonder what might have happened. But, amazingly, he knew he didn't care. It was frightening to have so utterly given up, the wind rushing by the car was fierce and howling, the metal frames and glass of the doors icy cold, and the black land outside devoid of any recognizable characteristics, a land of utter sterility. They swooped around, tires screeching, a big curve, and spread out to their left was Santa Fe. They slowed, abruptly, to the speed limit of 45 as they wheeled into the city limits. You didn't make it after all, did you, you motherfucker! he shouted, hilarious, at the driver. He took a long drink of the rye and handed the bottle to M. He laughed, and choked on the whisky, spit it into his lap. He was choking and roaring with laughter, and then M began to laugh, too. They swung into the main street of the town, hysterical, the driver still hunched over the wheel, then he, unwillingly, also began to laugh. He didn't make it after all, M said. The motherfucker! And gagged, laughed, the tears in his eyes, the laughter of the others in chorus with his. They were alive.

Needles, California

As a child, one of his great desires, a romantic dream, had been to cross the country on a streamliner, with plenty of money for a room and for the dining and club car. Now he sat in the comfortable seat above the lounge, in the Domeliner, looking out the window at the endless desert stretching away in blackness. He sipped his drink and lit another cigarette. It was so stupid, now, to be coming back. Why he was returning to New York was a matter unanswerable to him. To put up with his friends' pity, listen to their laughter as they tried to make him "forget." Ridiculous. At the front of the car was a small group of young air force men, very young. They sat with four or five girls, laughing and talking, boasting. At any other time he would have thought of them as unfortunate, matching his own army experiences with theirs. Now, they made him feel terribly lonely, completely removed from all human warmth, all human affection. The desert was implacable, the train moved slowly through Needles, where, the porter had told him, they would move into another time zone and lose an hour. An hour later, which meant to him, grotesquely, that he had been moved forward an hour from that time when his wife had told him that she was leaving him. He finished his drink and pushed the bell for the waiter, who came up the small stairway that led from the lounge and bar, and took the order, returned in a moment with it and noted the drink on his tab. He was probably drunk, he thought, but he didn't know whether he was or not. He didn't feel drunk, he didn't feel at all sleepy, the mere thought, in fact, of returning to his roomette and getting into bed disgusted him. He would never sleep on this train, but he would have to stop drinking soon, the lounge wasn't open all night: he had a pint, but it was another day and a half to Chicago, and he would have to save some whisky, he thought, I have to save some booze in case . . . in case, what? He didn't know what, but he'd save it. It was the one thing he possessed now that had any meaning to him at all. He could get out of it whenever he wanted. His grandmother's money could buy that. He drank again, and listened to the young airmen singing and then to the laughter of the girls. He wanted to join them but he was so old, he felt so absurdly old. And all he wanted was one of the girls anyway. Fuck *them*! Join them, for what? But if he could get one of those girls to his roomette . . . an old drunk, stupid. Even my wife wouldn't let me fuck her, and I expect to get *girls*? About now, he thought, about now, they must have rented a place in San Antonio. Did the children miss him? His beautiful children, whom he never saw in Mexican sunlight, whom he let go, with her and with him, and with his car . . . he looked quickly toward the group at the end of the car, afraid that they would somehow discover what a fool he was, what an imbecile. To let the man who had cuckolded him have his car! To listen, calmly, to his wife tell him that she hadn't loved him for five years, that all his friends had been to bed with her, she was sorry, she just had to do it, she didn't love him. Hadn't he even seen it, once? Why didn't he *know*! How could he have lived with her and not known how she was leaping into their arms—almost, she said, as if he brought them home, let them stay on as visitors for that very purpose. A pimp, unawares.

But what shook him, deeply, what really upended his life, opened his flesh almost, was the suspicion that his friends, whom he had thought were come, all those years, to see *him*, were actually present, there in his house, to see her. It was not the fact of his cuckolding that hurt so much as the fear that these friends had come, primarily, to make love to his wife, secondarily, incidentally almost, to see him. All the years that he believed that his friends had come to see him out of a need for him, an admiration for him, were now empty of any value, save the spurious one of bitter memory. He could not in his mind seem to find one pure instance which would now prove that they had come for him; their friendship with him was impossible to distinguish from their lust for her. It was suddenly to realize that five years of his life had been no more important than garbage. He put his glass down and walked down the stairs to the lounge to pay his bar bill. Two quiet men, in their sixties, sat across a table from each other, neither of them speaking. They didn't look at him as he walked past them into the corridor. They must be, he thought, the two brothers the porter told me about. Their mother was in a coffin in the baggage car and they were taking her home to Missouri to bury her. Come to sunny California, he smiled to himself, and die, totally aware of his bathetic pose yet enjoying it. He locked the door of his roomette, took a slug of the bourbon, lit a cigarette, and began to read *The New Yorker*.

Brooklyn, New York

They sat across from each other in the summer garden, the cool wind from the bay moving the leaves. There's no point in staying here any longer, he said. Just a while. Why don't you have another beer? *I'd* like another glass, she said. Beer, he said. For Christ sake. O.K. He called the waiter and pointed to the pitcher. It isn't that bad for you, is it? she said. I don't know, he said. I don't know how I feel about it. How can you be so damn cool about it? The waiter came with another pitcher of beer and he poured a glass for himself and one for her. Well? How can you? And you don't care? You *don't* care. Because you never gave a goddamn. That's a lie, she said. You know that? He finished his beer and poured himself another glass. I thought you wanted one, he said. She looked over at him and then away in the general direction of the water. Let's go down to the pier, she said. The pier, he said. For Christ sake, what are we going to do on the pier? Let's, she said. Let's walk. She sipped at her beer, then proffered the glass to him. Do you want to finish mine? No, he said, getting up and reaching for her coat. They walked down the street and onto the pier, past the ferry slips and out beyond the lights of the waiting room. At the end of the pier she sat down on the old wooden tug pilings. He took out a cigarette for her, and then for himself, lit them. You bitch, he thought, you whore. Her face was soft in the glow from the cigarette as she drew on it, and he looked at her for a minute, smoking. You bitch, he yelled, and struck her, knocking the cigarette from her mouth. She sat, her hands folded in her lap. I was waiting, she said. What? he yelled, what? I was waiting. Bitch! He struck her again and she began to bleed from the mouth. I'm sorry, she said. Oh, I'm sorry, he said, I'm sorry. He took out his handkerchief and wiped at the blood, then gave her his cigarette and lit another one for himself. The whole thing is so goddamned stupid, he said. Isn't it stupid, she said. Is it because you just had to do it, you just had to? he said. Yes, she said, I suppose so, I love *you*, though, I love you. She began to cry and he stroked her hair uselessly. Don't cry, he said. It's all right, I love you. She looked up at him. I'm so sorry, she said, I'm so sorry. O.K., he said, O.K. What do you say we go up and talk about it and have a *good* drink? All right, she said. She got up and smoothed her skirt and he took her hand. They walked slowly off the pier. It smells like rain, he said. Don't you think? She nodded and squeezed his hand.

Taos, New Mexico

The move to Taos was completed and they more or less settled in during the first two days. There was plenty of room, notwithstanding the visitors' needs, and the beauty, the bald, uncompromising space of the place impressed their Eastern and urban sensibilities. The second day that they were there, M decided to find out about wood for the fireplaces in the house, the small stock in the shed outside the front door noticeably depleted after only two nights and one day here, the weather now steadily cold. At just about the moment that M, the husband, and the driver were about to go into Taos to inquire about wood, two people who had known the previous tenants of the house arrived in a pickup truck with at least a half load of piñon, split and ready for the small, semioval fireplaces in the house. Everyone shook hands and M invited them into the house for drinks, after which they all joined in emptying the wood, and storing it in the small shed. The men told M that they cut their piñon every three weeks up in the mountains, working all day for a good supply, and that the next time they went they'd call for him to go with them. They were not natives, but had come here for different reasons from the Midwest. One was a painter and the other a writer, and during the ten days or so that the husband stayed on with M and R, he got to know them better, drinking with them or driving around the countryside while they pointed out landmarks and houses to M, introduced him to other inhabitants and houses. They were strange men, it seemed to the husband, helpless, finally, for all their gestures at freedom. The painter had an almost obsessive concern with highway

billboards and was in "league" with two or three other men—a
league which was dedicated to sawing down the billboards, defacing
them, or in any other way possible, ruining the Santa Fe and Albuquerque advertisers' attempts at commercialization of the area. It
seemed fairly laudable to the husband until he became aware that
Taos was, for all its "frontier" paraphernalia, its beautiful old
adobes, its primeval mountain ranges, a thriving art community, the
streets of the small town lined with art galleries which sold bad paintings of the mountains and clouds to rich Texas and Oklahoma vaca-
tioners. The painter was one of those artists who daubed all winter
long so that he might sell his work for staggering prices in the summer. There was a gruesome kind of pathology at work here, so the
husband thought; but he said nothing—the man was pleasant
enough. The other was a novelist whose first book had done rather
well, going into paperback and ultimately being bought by Holly-
wood. He worked as a sign painter's assistant now for seventy-five
cents an hour, the thirty or thirty-five thousand dollars he had made
on the book gone in a couple of years. His wife took trips to San
Francisco and Dallas to buy clothes, and shipped large "surreal"
paintings by air to those 10th Street galleries in New York which
would show her work as "repayment" for the gifts of money she sent
to help out with rent, etc. Invariably the paintings were returned, at
her expense. So the money had disappeared. The writer, however,
seemed to accept it all as a kind of game, and even joked about his
wife's squandering of his earnings. The husband held what he knew
was contempt in abeyance, since whatever "arrangements" he himself had made with his wife over the years were surely no more careful, and no less uxorious.

So their time in Taos passed, calmly enough. His nightly tensions
with his wife had almost ceased, since he made it a practice now to sit
up late with M in front of the fireplace in the living room, drinking
and talking of New York: they spoke of it, in fact, as though it no
longer existed, had been wiped out. His relations with his wife were
absolutely superficial, his status as a husband had passed into an area
of exaggerated memories of eroticism, sweeter to him as they be-

came more hyperbolic. His relations with the driver became somewhat as they had been years before, since he no longer thought of
him as a rival, but as a probable replacement. Further, his feelings
concerning the forced move which he felt the driver must soon make
had the effect of implanting in him a sense of irresponsibility as to
the final disposition of his marriage. In a word, he felt free, although
he knew that this visit had much to do with it. It gave him great
pleasure to see others struggling with their marriages, their very
lives, a feeling of rapport with them. A totally happy marriage would
have chagrined him. For some time, privately, he even toyed with
the idea of renting a house, here, in Taos. To be so surrounded by
the emotionally infirm would have pleased him, steadied him . . .
and he could always point out the windows to the beauty and majesty
of the mountains as his excuse for remaining. The driver would
leave, and he and his wife would smash each other to pieces, a shard
a day, until nothing was left. Then they could separate, and blame
each other. But these feelings were not, at the time, so coherent as all
this in him. He still gave lip service to the validity of preserving their
life together, of not making any move at all.

Finally they left. He spoke to M alone for a moment and pressed
fifty dollars on him, until he could "get straightened out." They got
into the car, and waving and laughing, and promising letters from
San Francisco and Mexico, drove off, down the road, to head south
to Albuquerque, then west to Arizona.

Gallup, New Mexico

He was, surprisingly, happy once they were back in the car: it
seemed a welcome resumption of what was fast becoming in his
mind the unavoidable. Ever since New Orleans, when he had felt the
spurious hope that things *could* right themselves, the journey was
simply a waiting for him. How sad it was, how unbearably sterile and
sad that it was impossible for either him or her to bring it out to the
light; they hovered about it, each night in bed with her was a torture

of mute recriminations, a strained silence made manifest in the feigned sleep, the quiet breathing of their two loveless bodies. He had given up all memory of "home," had given up the idea that it even had existed. His self-imposed blindness to what he now allowed himself to consider were her probable acts of infidelity seemed ugly to him in the light of what that blindness had led to, this insane trip, the irrational yet painstaking plans for it. Yet he was happy, now that they had passed through Albuquerque, and were heading west toward the Arizona border. The sky was heavy again, and 10 miles or so out of the city, a sloppy and splattering rain had begun, sloshing across the windows of the car, darkening the earth about them, slowing the erratic movements of the tumbleweeds that raced across the road in front of them, or kept pace with them for some distance before veering off the road into the red clay on either side of it. They stopped once, as it was growing dark, the rain heavier, the air colder, at a roadside tavern so that the children could go to the bathroom. Outside were three yellow buses filled with Indian women and children, and on the porch were other silent women, their children moving quietly about them. Inside the place the tables were filled with Indian men, most of them in faded blue overalls, black Stetsons, and, settled about each one's shoulders, a cheap pink or blue cotton blanket; they were all drunk and talking quietly, and as he walked in with the children and his wife, the room fell silent. Embarrassed, he ushered the children toward the rest rooms, then waited with his wife in the center of the room. The Indians investigated them calmly, drinking steadily, but making no sound. The children finally emerged and the four left, and as they entered the rain again the voices began. The women looked at them as they helped the children climb into the back of the station wagon, continued to look as they pulled away. The husband smiled back at them, but it was not felt, it was something to do. He had been judged, he felt, here in a country he knew nothing of—judged and somehow found wanting. They knew, he was certain, of their bleak lives, his stupid and impossible plan to move. The men had said nothing, had not looked at her, but at him. What kind of man is this? is what they had thought. He had never felt so out of touch with the past as now; the past had never happened, he was here, in the middle of alien land, patching and puttering, unaware of what had broken, or where. How long was it since there had *been* something to break? He was trying to repair an event, a congeries of events, with the useless aid of space, and they knew it, they gazed at him and they judged.

Fifty miles before Gallup they turned on the heater and soon after the rain turned to snow, light at first, but growing increasingly heavier. The radio said that it was snowing very heavily in Arizona, which meant that they were driving directly into it. There was no point in stopping at any of these little towns through which they passed, so they figured they'd try for Gallup, then spend the night there. The snow became heavier, and the driving slower. Five miles outside Gallup they saw the first snowplows moving past them, heading east, and they moved forward, the gain of each yard now imperative. Finally, they saw the lights of Gallup before them, blurred in the whirling snow, and they parked on the main street in front of a Mexican restaurant.

They ordered food and ate hungrily, although the children complained that the chili was too hot. He tipped the waitress too much, illogical in his gratitude for shelter and food, and she smiled warmly at them all, and helped his daughter on with her coat. Outside, the snow was beginning to pile up in drifts, and they got into the car and moved slowly down the street, looking for a place to stay. Before they had reached the next corner, they found one, called the Log Cabin Motel, a group of private, detached cabins and a deep shed for vehicles. They drove in immediately, and he made arrangements for the night.

He sat in the semidark by the window and smoked, staring out at the courtyard, the sweeping snow that moved across it. Everyone else was asleep, and the quiet was intense. He put out his cigarette and got up, moved aimlessly about the room, then walked to his wife quickly, stood staring down at her face, then reached out and touched her cheek. She stirred, and moved her hand, heavily, over her face. He took off his undershorts and T-shirt and got into bed beside her, his face pinched and tight as he held his breath. He moved close to her and put his hand out, touched her thigh. She was still. He thought, please, please, Jesus, please, I don't care if she loves me or not, please. His hand felt heavy to him, and hot, resting on her thigh, and he moved it up until he could feel the heat from her crotch; it seemed impossibly hot, and he felt his blood pumping in the ear that he had pressed into the pillow. He took a deep breath and moved his fingers into her pubic hair and she stirred, and groaned, then made a motion away from him. He was filled with terror and lifted his hand away. The covers seemed like tons against the back of his hand, and he breathed slowly, his hand suspended, his forearm and shoulder beginning to ache. She lay still again, and he put his hand back on her, moved his fingers tentatively, then nuzzled his face into her hair, darling, baby, he whispered. She opened her eyes and looked at him for a moment, frightened, then reached down swiftly and pulled his hand from her. You dirty bastard, she said. You sneaky, dirty bastard. Please, he said, please, I can't stand it. She moved about in the bed and turned her back on him. Go jerk off, she said. He lay back in bed, his emotions splintered, his face flushed and burning, his hand helplessly stroking his swollen penis. He got out of bed, finally, and lit another cigarette, then locked himself in the bathroom, and, in the dark, obeyed her. When he returned to the bed she was asleep again, her face calm.

They left early the next morning, the snow having stopped sometime during the night, the roads cleared now, the patches left on the land brilliant against the red earth. For a time, they had been concerned over the fact that the brakes had frozen during the night, but after working on the car for an hour or so, the driver got them into operation again, and they set out, traveling due west toward Arizona, the sky clear and blue, and the air a dry, numbing entity in which one suddenly realized the cold after a considerable time during which it hardly seemed to matter. It was a treacherous sort of cold, flat and primeval as the earth, a being of enormous power and one which held sway along with the space it filled. If anything, the land was more sparse, more flat than it had been in central New

Mexico, no mountain ranges in sight, merely the endless road flat and black through the land. He stared ahead of him, listening to the children talk in the back; the snow seemed to have revived them, seemed somehow to be a recognizable link with the reality which they had left behind in New York. It was something identifiable to them, he thought, even though it lies on this alien land . . . and anything that would make them feel better met with his approval now, he catered to their every whim, spoiled them shamelessly. His wife said nothing about this, and it seemed obvious to him that she felt the same twinges he did concerning their (what seemed now) cruel treatment of the children. He had consoled himself as long as possible with the thought that *he* was their father and so what he said was good for them, was indeed, so. But the children lately seemed so bewildered, not only as it had been at the start of the trip, by the endless travel, but recently by the more frequent and extended stops they made with friends—as just past, with M and R. They had stayed so long with them that the children had grown used to Santa Fe and Taos, had grown used to the other children. At precisely the moment that they felt most "at home," the trip had resumed. All he could say to them now was how beautiful Mexico would be, how they would all go swimming every day, how they would learn to speak Spanish—all the sad deception he so easily fed their minds; although, he protested to himself, if they never reached Mexico, it would be not his fault, but hers. He awaited her declaration, not dreaming that it ever really would be made, hoping that somewhere between this grim and lifeless country and San Francisco, some miracle of love would occur so that she would be to him as he now imagined her to have been before they left New York. It was imperative to his sanity that he invent occasions of affection that had not been real since before the birth of his son; so, bizarrely, the trip became exactly what it had not been at its inception, a flight from established happiness and comfort.

They crossed the Arizona border before noon and headed for the Painted Desert and the Petrified Forest: they had been told that at this time of year both places were empty of the usual crowd of tourists, and that they weren't to be missed. They were, at least, *places* to go to, they were on maps, they existed as demarcated areas of barrenness within the barrenness which surrounded them. He turned and began to tell the children about the Petrified Forest. The car moved swiftly on, his wife expressionless behind her sunglasses, the driver dialing the radio for music. You protect your children anyway, he thought. He didn't realize that he was using them, the fact of their existence, as an occasion for not facing what was to be inevitable, his loss of them.

Painted Desert, Arizona

He stood, his daughter in his arms, looking down at the desert, pink, blue, black, spread out before them to the horizon. The wind was bitter cold, and he shivered and held his daughter closer, adjusted the hood of her winter jacket. His son, his wife, and the driver were just specks below as they climbed about on the enormous pink and rust rocks, followed the crevasses between them. He waited, trying to interest his daughter in their adventures, but they were too far away, their cavorting had nothing to do with her, and for him, too, they seemed unreal. He could see their gestures of excitement as they rounded huge slabs of pink rock to come upon flat sandy glades of black or blue, but their laughter was unheard. All he could hear was the wind in his ears, it howled and knifed at his clothes. His daughter began to whimper and he turned then and walked back to the car and put her on the front seat, climbed in beside her. He turned on the ignition and started the heater, lit a cigarette. He didn't like this place. He missed now, terribly, water. He needed to see water, San Francisco seemed to him to beckon with a mysterious beauty simply because it sat facing the sea. This Painted Desert was too vast, he hated the petrified beauty of its colors, the pastel shades merging and blending in the dazzling sun, the pinkish haze of the horizon. He reached into the glove compartment and gave his daughter a piece of chocolate, and she sat quietly, eating, both of them warm now, the sun bright and comfortable on his neck.

After about fifteen minutes they came up to the car, laughing and out of breath and he thought how natural they looked together, how happy. Putting himself in the driver's place, he imagined his some-what severe face, the reserve in it: he was so old now, he'd spent his life working while the driver roamed Europe, he was too aloof, too uninterested, to even go climbing down into the edge of the desert, this fantastic desert, with his son. Let her go, he thought. They opened the doors of the car, and he smiled at his son. How was it? he said. Neat, the boy said, it was neat, daddy. But we got all out of breath. Yes, his wife said, the air is really thin, I guess. I didn't think I'd make it back up for a minute. Baloney, the driver said. You're a real Tenzing—well, how about the Petrified Forest, he said. You kids like to see trees six million years old? Yes, yes, his daughter said, clapping her hands. Neat, his son said. They got the kids settled in the back of the car, resumed their usual seats, and started to move out of the little space behind the guard rail. As they swept around to get back on the road, he looked for a moment at the desert below, seeming to see the three figures, still, far off toward the horizon. He turned around swiftly and tousled his son's hair, lightly and playfully clipped his daughter's chin with his fist. Couple of wild Westerners, he said. His heart felt large and there was a pain in his chest as he fumbled around for his sunglasses. Patches of snow, as white and fine as salt, crunched underneath the tires.

Petrified Forest, Arizona

Beautiful, but dead, he thought, but the colors! The stone, almost like marble, of the petrified and fallen trees took on incredible hues in the bright sunlight, scatterings of what seemed at first to be peb-bles turned out to be chunks of the same petrified wood, flung about on the ground in thousands. They stopped the car many times, getting out to handle the wood, look at the beautifully clear grains, still defined precisely after the millions of years. The children couldn't believe that these huge broken cylinders were once trees and he almost shared their disbelief—they seemed almost manufactured, they were too perfect. Although there were signs all about the roads, as well as in the Information Building that they had passed through, enjoining all visitors not to take away pieces of the wood as souvenirs, he couldn't resist, and so took three pieces which he selected for their beauty of shape and color, and their grain. It was, he knew, partly because they had small pieces of the wood for sale in the souvenir shop, along with shiny blue-black stones called Aztec eyes: this gross and hypocritical injunction not to take the wood, but to buy it, was part of the reason, the other part being that he felt a need to take from this place something to give his children, something to prove that they had really been here, and not simply customers in another souvenir shop. The painful aspect of this decision was to come later, when he commanded his children not to say anything about the wood hidden in their laundry bag when they were stopped at the exit from the preserve by a guard who simply asked them whether or not they had any pieces of wood in their possession. He lied, smoothly, and looked behind at the children as they pulled away; they were quiet, and looked at him, knowing that he had lied, and wondering about his lie—and he had taken the wood for them, he had told himself. To implicate them in his petty theft, perhaps, was more like it, to make them feel some of the misery that he felt? But that was too heartless. Whatever he had done it for, it was done, he had made his own children accomplices in this picayune act, they didn't understand it, but they obeyed. He gave them chocolate, and tried to hold their attention on the blue and pink mesas that they headed toward in the distance, a landscape of some foreign planet.

The road wound between these enormous mesas, one more magnificent than the other, and he had a sudden desire to climb one, get to the top and overlook this dead landscape, so they stopped the car and he got out, ran toward the base of a huge pink and black mesa, turned to look at the car, a small green toy back on the road, then

started to climb. It was easier than he thought, the texture of the
mesa not rocky and hard, but yielding, as if it had been made of
ashes, clinkers. His feet sank in a little with each step and he kept
moving steadily upward, until he stood at the top. Below, the car was
the size of a roach, green, the glinting sun off the roof dazzling to his
eyes. His children played about, picking up pieces of petrified coral,
shells, ancient corpses from a world of water. The wind screamed in
his ears, and he waved down at them, but they didn't see him; he
could see his wife's legs out the door of the car, and he waved again
and called, but no one looked up. He turned then and faced the way
they had come: the road was empty of traffic, the desert stretched
away to the horizon, these huge and eerie constructions the only
windbreak for hundreds of miles. It was getting terribly cold, and
the sun had the buttery glow of late afternoon, the land was weird.
He called out to the wilderness, some gibberish, then called again,
the wind cold and fierce in his open mouth, the membrane drying
instantly. He turned again to face the road and saw his son waving to
him from behind the car. Far in the distance, a gigantic white cloud
stretched flat across the sky, bending with the curve of the earth. He
started down, almost in panic, filled with an unrecognizable fear, a
choking sense of his own loneliness and failure.

Arizona

The third failure, he thought, although this one was perhaps con-
scious, out of his disgust, his annoyance with me. They were on the
shoulder of the road, desert all about them, out of gas. The nearest
town was two miles away, so the husband got a gallon gas can out of
the floor trunk and started toward the town, the light thin now, and
the wind getting colder as the night came on. He went himself to get
away from the car, to get away from all of them, at least for a while.
After about fifteen minutes of walking, he turned around and saw
the car far behind him. He could keep going, couldn't he? He had his
traveler's checks, and could keep going, spare them all further mis-

eries. But he smiled at this, how ridiculous it was. A car passed him
and stopped a few yards ahead, and a young man leaned out the
window as he came abreast of the car. That your car back there, out
of gas? Yeah, he said. Get in, the man said, swinging open the door.
His wife moved toward her husband and he got in, put the gas can in
the back. A hell of a place to get stuck, he said. You bet, the man said,
you're lucky it's not late, everything in this town ahead closes at ten.
You come from New York? Yeah, he said, and paused. Got a job
waiting on the Coast, San Francisco, he lied. He didn't know why he
lied, but there was a deep sense of shame in him concerning his
leisure, even here with this stranger. Or was he ashamed of the fact
that he was on the road with his family and another man. He lied,
that's my wife and kids, and my brother. We had a lot of trouble in
New York, and we heard that they need men in a new aircraft factory
in Frisco. In San Francisco? the man said. That's a new one on me,
most of the plants are in Southern Cal, around L.A. Well, yeah, the
husband said, that's what I meant. He was angry now and embarrassed. We're going to stay with some friends in San Francisco, and
look for work south, but like, work out of Frisco. Yeah, the man said,
I guess that's a good idea, but there's nothing in San Francisco itself,
far as I know, we were there just last month, visiting my wife's folks.
His wife smiled.

They reached the town, a huddle of frame buildings, a motel, a
supermarket, a bowling alley, a tavern, and a service station, and the
man pointed to the station. There's where you want to go, he said,
and opened the door for him. Thanks a lot, he said, for the lift. That's
O.K., buddy, he said. Good luck to you. They waved and he went
into the station and bought a gallon of gas. The old man took his
money, gave him change. You stuck fur, son? No, about two miles
back on the road. That was all. He hefted the can and started back
down the road, the shadows long and purple now, the mesas in the
distance blurred in the soft light. Far to the east the sky was already
dark blue, but to the west, behind him, it was still a bright blue-
yellow. He trudged down the road, walking easily, the can swinging.
In a culvert at the side of the road he saw something furry, stopped

and looked to discover that it was the body of a large wolf, its muzzle bloody, the side of its body caved in. He put the gas down and looked around him for a moment, crossed the road, and found a stick. It was light and brittle, but it gave him a sense of security. He saw, far away, the green blur that was the car, and he walked faster toward it, the dust swirling from the desert floor in circles. He thought he heard a howl, and looked behind him, walking steadily. The son of a bitch could've at least offered to go instead of me. And that son of a bitch could've given me a lift back, two fucking miles! He spat on the macadam, the weight of the can beginning to annoy him. Some driver, running out of gas in the middle of a goddamn desert! Shit! He switched the can and stick from one hand to the other, walked on, the car beginning to take on more precise contours. He wanted to blame the driver for doing this on purpose, but he knew that was a first step toward losing whatever control he still possessed over this journey. We'll be in Frisco in a week, he thought. I can make it till then without going completely goofy. Let them have their fun, the fucks! For a moment he thought of dropping the can, "accidentally," just as he reached the car, but laughed at himself. We'll never get to Grand Canyon at that rate, tonight, he thought . . . and it was getting bitter cold. He could hear his wife and children singing, and the driver waved at him. He lifted his stick in return. You assless bastard, he said, suddenly delighted with the phrase.

Grand Canyon, Arizona

They had taken a wrong turn at a crossroads, so were moving parallel to the road that would lead them to the South Rim of the Canyon. It was almost completely dark now, so they decided that they might as well stop and eat, before making the swing that would put them onto the right road. They found a restaurant, large, bright, and clean, with white tablecloths, and went in, the driver carefully locking the car against the Hopis that squatted in front of the restaurant, blanketed and sombreroed. The food was good, brook trout and fresh vegetables, baked potatoes and hot rolls, and they ate quickly, wanting to get to the Canyon before it got too late, so that they could check into a lodge there in time for a good night's sleep, and a look at the Canyon in the morning before heading west to Las Vegas. They finished, the husband paid the check, and they went outside to the car, the children looking curiously at the Indians. The husband felt strangely drawn to them, they were placid, they sat in the dark and cold wind, silently, looking at the car with guarded eyes, simply waiting out their lives, it seemed. The Indians sat, time apparently meaningless to them. Was it? They were so at home in this brutally brilliant land, this endless country; while he was intimidated by it all, had been intimidated since Texas. He never thought he could ever want to see a city, alive, dirty, ugly, as badly as he now wanted to, thought of Las Vegas with a desire so acute that it was almost a pain in his throat. They were settled in the car now, the Indians still watching, immobile, the car's brights sweeping across them, their eyes glinting for a moment, then they were on the road, moving swiftly north toward the Canyon. He looked at the fuel gauge and saw that it registered a third full, sat back and lit a cigarette. That ought to be enough to make it, he thought. But it wasn't, and, later, on the curving, treacherous road that led along the Canyon's rim, a road covered with ice and frozen snow, the impossible happened: 20 miles from the little community of Grand Canyon where there was waiting gas station, food, and lodging, the driver turned to him and said, we won't make it all the way. The fury that rose in him was so great, of such sheer paranoid intensity, that he inadvertently groaned, then rescued his self-betrayal with a short laugh. Somebody'll come along, the driver said. But they had seen no other car for at least 50 miles.

Jacksontown, Ohio

It was almost sunset, the luminous yellow light of the fall bathing them, as they got out of Eddy's pickup truck at the edge of the state preserve two or three miles outside of Jacktown: the car would be

ready by evening and Eddy had loaned them his truck so that they
could get out of the hotel room for a few hours, and he had suggested
that they ride out to the Indian mounds at the edge of town. They
got out of the truck after parking it under rapidly thinning trees, and
scuffed their way through heaps of crackling red and brown leaves
toward the mounds, preserved beautifully by the State of Ohio, but
apparently never visited. The immediate neighbors were uncu-
rious, and this area of Ohio was obviously devoid of tourists at any
time of year—so the mounds were almost inviolate, silent, the leaves
moving above them, falling crisply, rapidly, in the gusts of chill wind
from the west.

There were two separate precincts—one, a small one, roughly
rectangular, leading into a large area, a pentagon, the sides of which
were perfectly shaped hillocks beneath which lay the dust of hundreds of primitive Indians. The area in the middle was almost wind-
less, dotted by a few enormous beech and oak trees, placed haphaz-
ardly in the middle of a huge lawn of soft grass, now rusty and
parched in spots. They walked about, and he tried to explain to the
children that this was an Indian burying ground, a cemetery, led
them along atop one of the sides of the pentagon, the three of them
walking single file, away on the other side of the lawn, his wife and
the driver walking parallel to them upon another mound. His son
rushed then, with a whoop, down the mound onto the lawn and
galloped across it, losing his footing and falling, laughing, shouting,
as his daughter followed, then leaped on the boy, and both of them
then rolling, tumbling over in the grass.

His wife and the driver had turned back the other way now, and
were sitting at the point where one arm of the pentagon joined another, a few yards away from the entrance to the smaller rectangular
area. Just at this point stood two gigantic trees, one on either side of
the small corridorlike opening which joined the two preserves—the
light moved in their branches as the wind picked up, it glittered and
shuddered on the grass, the sounds of his children's voices were remote and indistinct, the smoke from his wife's cigarette suddenly
stood out, dazzling white as it moved into a shaft of sunlight. He was
totally alone, here with these moldered bones, the world lay outside

the trees, here there was simply silence, the edged cold of fall and thin sunlight. His children disappeared between the two trees and into the adjoining area, his wife and the driver followed them, he saw her face suddenly, a pale cameo, turned in profile toward him as she laughed at something the driver had said. The sun went suddenly behind a high, banked cloud and the grove was plunged into a spectral greyness. He straightened up from his stoop and hurried down the slope of the mound, trotted, then ran toward the trees at the far end of the lawn, the leaves crunching underneath his feet, a panic of terror in him, as he ran hard as he could now, in a straight line, dead in the center of the pentagon, as far away from the surrounding mounds as he could be. He was prepared to see the space beyond the trees empty of all save fallen leaves, and ran the last yards, panting, stumbling. He didn't want to be here, alone, he didn't belong with the dead yet.

Grand Canyon, Arizona

The forest ranger's shack at the entrance to Grand Canyon National Park was empty when they arrived there, but a light was burning inside, and outside a small sign hung on a chain. It said: DANGER ICY ROAD, but they drove past, no place to go now except to Grand Canyon, which was a drive of 40 miles through this park, along twisting roads, covered, if the sign were true, with ice. He knew that their gas must be low, glancing surreptitiously at the gauge, but hoped that they'd have enough to make it all the way. What would happen if they ran out here, on this absolutely deserted road, was a possibility so unpleasant that he refused to think about it. The driver gazed ahead, the car moving now at about 35 or 40 miles an hour, the road beginning already to twist and turn, the headlights picking up masses of trees and brush on either side of them. After about 10 minutes or so, just as they took a turn at the bottom of a hill, they hit a patch of ice and the rear wheels shot out to the right while the driver fought for control, finally brought the car around again and continued on.

They laughed weakly, shortly, the children were awake in the back, and he looked around at them, said something about the park, how huge it was, some ridiculous thing to hide his fear of this night, this road. For a moment, as they skidded on the ice, the headlights had pointed straight out over the shoulder of the road, into air only, nothing but black, freezing air, and he realized that there, perhaps 20 yards or less from them, was the lip of the Canyon itself, below— what was it—a mile? the Colorado River, a simple silver thread, a sickening drop of a mile to that sluggish water. And there, too, the weather a weird 65 degrees or so, while here on the road it was so cold that the air and wind outside the car seeped in, chilling them, despite the roaring heater.

They had gone perhaps half the way when they all heard the engine cough for a second, cough again, then pick up again in its steady drone. He looked at the driver who said, we won't make it all the way. I'll try to get as much out of it as I can . . . and so started coasting down hills wherever possible, his foot coaxing the brake pedal as they slid, wheels locked and useless over what seemed to be increasingly frequent slabs of ice, thick now, and white. They covered another two or three miles this way, the driver steering methodically, while the husband bent over an AAA map, figuring their distance from the town of Grand Canyon. He had just determined that it was at least 15 more miles when the engine coughed again, and the driver pumped the gas pedal rhythmically, the engine coughing again, again, then suddenly there was no sound and they swooped up a last hill, then down, gaining perhaps another two or three hundred yards, the car rolling finally to a stop, the driver pulling it over to the shoulder of the road. Well, he said. Somebody'll come along. We hope, the husband said. His wife was silent, the children sat in the back, a blanket around them, staring out at the blackness of trees and thin air. The driver reached into the glove compartment and got a flashlight, opened his door, and stood, then, on the road, while he too, then, opened his door, followed him out.

As soon as he had shut the door he realized that they *had* to flag down a car, the air was so cold that he gasped, the wind numbed him

instantly through the heavy corduroy jacket he wore. They would be
sick if they stayed here all night, the children . . . it was impossibly
cold, impossibly lonely, the stars so clear that he could swear that he
saw them as the five-pointed, silver stars one gets in grade school, his
son, in fact, had them pasted in his first-grade composition book.
The driver had the flash on, pointed back the way they had come,
moving it up and down slowly, as a brakeman might. Jesus Christ,
it's cold, he said. The husband said, should we walk? but to himself,
and immediately realized that would be absurd, it would be danger-
ous on this road, 15 miles through this zero cold, and the forest, he
had read, was a wildlife preserve, who knows what would emerge
from those black clumps on either side of the road? His city-bred
fear was intense, he loathed this virginity of land, what good was it,
a goddamned hole in the ground, a goddamned forest with a road
through it—and, if they both went, what of her and the children in
the car, alone. The wind knifed at him, and he moved to the lee side
of the car, his hands shoved deep in his pockets.

How long they waited he couldn't tell, nor would he look at his
watch, the idea of time passing scared him. He thought that it must
be getting cold inside the car now and he looked at his wife and children, the three of them in the back now, huddled together under the
blanket. He smoked constantly, the tip of the cigarette a hope and a
reminder of warmth, thought that they could build a fire if someone
didn't come along soon. The driver had turned out the flash, waiting
now to see if a car would come before he turned it on to signal, he
stood opposite to him, to windward, his pants ballooning in the wind
that came crashing down on them in a steady torrent. The bastard!
In the wind, like he isn't cold, he thought. His fault, all of it, while
my wife and children freeze, and it's only . . . he looked at his watch,
a little after midnight. He was sorry immediately he had looked, the
full realization of what it would be like to spend the whole night here
suddenly confronting him in terms of time as well as space. And just
then, he saw headlights, coming the way they had come, not fast,
carefully, the car moving carefully, and he turned to the driver, but
he already had stepped out into the road and had the light on, moving

it up and down, carefully, letting the beam play directly onto the road, then up slightly into the air, at windshield level. Whoever it was would have to stop. It was, they saw, a moment later, a panel truck, inside was an Indian, a Hopi from the nearby reservation, his wife and son. The windows of the truck were open, the boy was in only a thin sweater, shivering, the woman in a cotton dress, the man in a faded levi jacket. He was maybe 30, handsome as Indians are, a feeling of wisdom in his slow look and actions as he leaned out the cab window. You stuck? he said. Yes, he said. The town's far, the Hopi said. They were all silent. It's goddamn cold. He looked up at the sky, then down again, at the husband. Can we siphon some gas from your tank, the driver said, I think maybe a half gallon, even less, would do it for us. The Indian looked at him and at the husband. You got a siphon, he said, a tube. The driver looked around, at the ground, looked at the husband, then said, I'll take the windshield wiper tube off, the air tube . . . that'll do it. We'll pay you, the husband said, to say something, to be helpful. He was delighted that the driver had thought of this expedient (he would never have thought of it) but annoyed that he was, indeed, indispensable. An incredible emotion of paranoia moved through him, he had the evanescent thought that the driver had done it all, everything, the lemon of a car, the running out of gas, all the troubles they had had, so that he *would* be indispensable . . . to prove it to his wife, prove he was so much more a man than he; the assless bum!

He had the hood up and, now, had the wiper tube in his hand; the Hopi had his gas cap off and the driver was sucking gas out, the gallon can between his feet. He coughed, gagged, and he saw the stream of red gas gush from the tube, heard it splash, then pour steadily, into the can. The Indian looked on, silently. When the can was half full, the driver stopped, glanced at the Indian, then hefted the can, and handed the flash to the husband. Hold it, he said. He poured into their tank, kept a little, then moved to the open hood and poured it directly on the dried-out carburetor, the husband following with the flash. You need more than that, I think, the Hopi said, you got 15, 16 miles. Yeah, the driver said, I guess, I don't know what I was thinking. He repeated the process, poured another half gallon into the tank, then got in the car, and started it. The engine turned over, wheezing, a few times, then caught, and he let it idle, got out and slammed the hood. The Hopi was climbing into his truck, his wife and son looked straight ahead, as they had done throughout the entire operation. The husband reached into his pocket and took out three singles, gave them to the Indian. Thanks a million, he said. The Hopi looked at the money, said, too much. But the husband said, not just for the gas, for—well, nobody came along, I mean you . . . the Hopi looked at the bills again, shrugged, then started the truck. He drove off, and they settled in the car, the driver had the heater on, and it was beginning to blow hot air. The husband settled back in the seat as they moved off, the taillights of the Indian's truck red pinpoints in the dark ahead.

The lodge that they chose to stay in was too handsome, and too expensive. He looked around the lobby, where an enormous fireplace threw out flickers of light from a giant log that burned steadily. In chairs and on sofas in front of the fire sat a group of perhaps 15 boys and girls in their teens, singing and drinking hot chocolate. The bellboy was bringing in their bags, and he was registering at the desk while the clerk looked at him with what he felt was distrust; he must have looked like a bum to him, here, at the Grand Canyon Lodge, in his baggy levis, old corduroy coat, his hair tousled and knotted from the wind, and, certainly, too long. They followed the bellboy up the stairs and went to their rooms, and immediately his wife undressed the children and gave them baths. He sat in an easy chair, looking around the room, smoking, feeling the warmth from the radiators move into him, rejuvenating him. The driver was down the hall, in a single, and their room was large, with twin double beds, crisp-sheeted and with heavy soft blankets. They put the children in bed and they were asleep almost immediately, while he and his wife sat in a soft light, quietly. What transients these kids have become, he thought, a different bed about every night, and they just go to sleep,

lights on, people in the room, it means nothing. He put out his cigarette, lit another, wondered if there was a bar downstairs. I'm going
to see if we can get a drink, he said, and got up, went out into the hall,
and down the stairs, his feet silent on the thick rug. When he got to
the lobby, the kids who had been in front of the fireplace were gone,
and the fire, itself, was banked. He went to the clerk, diffident, is
there a bar—open? The clerk smiled, said, sorry, sir, we close at
midnight. He smiled then, guilty that he should want a drink, apol-
ogized by saying, we ran out of gas on the road here . . . it was damn
cold. The clerk smiled. He smiled again, well, thanks, good night.
Good night, sir, the clerk said, oh sir, coffee and toast is served in
front of the fire from 8 to 9:30 in the morning. Thanks, he said,
thank you, good night. When he got back to the room, his wife was
in the shower, he took off his shirt and sat, smoking again, looking at
his children, expecting the driver to come in. But he didn't come.

His wife came out of the bathroom in her panties, her breasts bare,
and he got up and turned away from her, took off his T-shirt while
she got into bed. Oh, what beautiful sheets, she said. So crisp,
mmmm. She yawned and he went into the bathroom, took off his
clothes and turned on the shower, got into it, the hot water and steam
melting, thawing, the pillar of ice that seemed to stand upright,
tense, in the center of his body. Where did it all go wrong? he
thought, and immediately laughed, talked to the yellow and black
tiles of the shower stall, where, dahling, where did it go wrong, oh
my dahling, we were so happy once—in Vienna—before der var; he
laughed at himself and began to soap himself, then suddenly, he was
crying as freely as a child, he crouched on one knee on the floor of the
stall, weeping, the hot water splashing in needles on his back and
head, the soapsuds running, greyly dirty, in swirls around the drain.

They met the driver the next morning in the lobby, and, since it
was too late for coffee and toast gratis, they went to the lodge's restaurant, and ate a huge breakfast of pancakes, eggs, ham, coffee, rolls,
and coffee cake, then he paid their bill, and they loaded the car,
started out to see what there was to be seen here, at the Grand Can-

yon. The lodge, and all those near by, were virtually empty now, in early winter, and the roads corresponded. They drove back the way they had come for a few miles, properly exclaiming, now that the terror and blackness were over, of the "adventure" of the preceding evening; it was, of course, to become an occasion for anecdote in the future, he was already elaborating on it in his mind, they all laughed. But the edge of the Canyon, their present, and past, proximity to it, was very real. At one point, they pulled into a little area set aside for cars and sight-seers, perched out over the rim, guarded by a high wire fence, and they looked down. The depth of the thing was eerie to him, the children spoke of flying down, of going down all the way, and other things, while he looked, it was really unbelievable, like looking at New York from the Jersey salt flats, only vertically.

Later, they stopped at a souvenir shop and had atrocious hot chocolate in front of a magnificent fireplace, and he bought, before they left, a brilliantly painted, carved Hopi sun-god, a soft purple feather affixed to his head, his mask startling red and yellow against black, set it over the dashboard with Scotch tape when they returned to the car. They had had enough, but asked the children how they felt, did they want to stay? They were indifferent, so they started again, west, through Kaibab Forest, another wildlife preserve, looking now for deer, bear, whatever, the children looking out the rear window, the sun brilliant now, the temperature warmer. Everybody seemed rested, he was delighted, for their next stop was Las Vegas, a city. They could make it by dark. And then the last lap, to San Francisco, and then, to Mexico? She did seem better, who knows, and the driver's sullenness had almost vanished, maybe in San Francisco? He wanted to try, to keep trying, she had loved him, once, things were solvable, if they could free themselves, he thought, just move together as they had, at times, the bitterness was a symptom, certainly, not a cause, they could do it. But she was so remote, she moved in a box, transparent, but sealed. But Las Vegas was a city! And San Francisco, a city! The Hopi sun-god was garish in the light that streamed into the car, the desert was almost friendly. He turned on the radio.

Boulder City, Nevada

Because of the sun, the terrain seemed friendlier than it had for days although it was still desert, they drove for miles without seeing a town, then would come into one, fill the tank (about which they were very careful now), and continue on. It was getting dark, and they were still in Arizona, but were sure to make Vegas by nightfall. The land seemed to become more mountainous, at any rate, the car was alternately climbing and descending as they traveled, but it soon became apparent that they were going steadily down from high country, the darkness changed the irregular slabs of mountain and rock into huge monstrosities, all black now, without the sun to bring out their unworldly colors. Their ears were popping constantly, and his daughter was complaining that her ears hurt her, she began to whimper.

The night had come, fast, and they were still about 25 miles from the border and Hoover Dam, and his daughter was crying now, loud, his wife was annoyed with her, as was he, and he smoked constantly, nervously, his heart pumping in jagged rhythm as he listened to her whine. He turned to his wife, listen, he said, maybe she really has an earache, maybe you should go back with her and keep her ears warm, even my ears hurt—he turned around to his son, how are you, he said. I'm fine, dad, the boy said, just that my ears are popping. His daughter suddenly let out a piercing scream, and then another, she was in real pain, and their steady descent, he knew, would be murderous on her if she did have an earache. It was that night on the road, that goddamn cold weather, he said, but nobody paid attention to him, the car had picked up speed, as the driver bent over the wheel, moving faster now, down, down, to make the distance to Boulder City disappear as quickly as possible, his wife in the back, now holding their daughter in her lap, a blanket pressed over her right ear, rocking her back and forth, the little girl screeching with pain. I hope to Jesus there's a doctor we can find in that town, he said. The driver said, oh, sure, it's a pretty big town, we'll find someone open. They streaked through passes, around giant rocks, fat with darkness and shadows, his daughter's crying and screaming subsiding into steady sobs. They began then to see signs, HOOVER DAM, and directions, and in a few minutes were over the crest of a hill, looking down on a fantastically huge structure, white and ponderous, millions of gallons of water shimmered under its walls, light studded it, jewellike. It was something out of a science-fiction movie, or, what was that old movie, he thought, *Metropolis*. Weird and silent below, but over its road, along the top of the thickest wall, lay the town, and now he was grateful that they should be here, at this moment, because his daughter looked down at the dam, the lights, as his wife explained to her what it was; she was distracted momentarily.

Over the dam, and, miraculously, a sign that told them that the Boulder City Hospital was to the left. He said, go there, to the driver, and the car swung into the deserted, wide streets, the wind blowing hard here (did the wind never stop!) as always, swirls of desert sand covering the streets, pelting the windshield as fine rain. They got to the hospital and parked, he and his wife went in with his daughter, while the driver and son stayed in the car, in the parking lot. He carried her in the side entrance, she was crying again, seeing the hospital, his wife held his arm, how pathetic a gesture, together in his daughter's misery. They went in the Emergency Room entrance and his daughter's wailing brought a nurse out immediately, what seems to be the trouble, and they told her, an earache. A man appeared, in a suit, carrying a bag, and the nurse turned to him, Doctor . . . she began. I *was* leaving, nurse. He looked at them. Well come in, he said, come in, pointing to an examination room and preceding them. He was giving them a break! The doctor was really going to stay to treat a child in pain! But the husband held his tongue, he was grateful they had caught him still there. And what kind of emergency room could it be, that the doctors leave at 8 o'clock? His daughter sat on the table, wailing, her face red and wet, contorted by her pain and fear, and the doctor looked at her; meanwhile the nurse filled out a card with the answers the husband made, their name, occupation, and so on. When he said he lived in New York, she said, well, *you're* a long way from home, the doctor looking in his daughter's ear while his wife held her around the waist, stroked her hair. He wrote a prescription, said that they could get it filled right in town, it's a throat infection, he said, and her ear is affected. Then he left. The husband looked at the nurse, and picked up his daughter. She smiled at him, said twelve dollars, sir, and he paid her, got his change.

They moved swiftly through the wind to the car, then drove down the main street, his daughter quiet now, she said the pain was going away, but she sobbed occasionally. The drugstore was as big as a barn, he waited in the blinding fluorescence as the prescription was filled—a small bottle of orange fluid, one teaspoon every two hours, four fifty, thank you. In the car, they gave her the first dose immediately, and his wife held her as they moved out toward Vegas, the highway more crowded than they had seen it since Gallup, most of the cars headed west. Boulder City sprawled in neon on either side of the road for maybe 10 miles, then they were in pitch blackness again, moving steadily at 75 over, again, flat country. His daughter slept, his son sat between him and the driver, his head on the husband's arm. All this way waiting for Vegas, he thought, and now she's sick.

Las Vegas, Nevada

But if he had thought his daughter's sickness would affect his wife's plans, he was wrong, because as soon as they were in the motel his wife was looking through her things to see what dress she would wear for their night here. And what else should I expect? he asked himself. After all these years, that my wife will go one inch out of her way to accommodate someone else? His wife, who wouldn't call to say she would be late while someone waited for her, she was in her own isolation room, the rest of the world, so she assumed, was in its own. They had all been excited, even his daughter, as they saw Las Vegas in the distance. After miles of blackness, nothing in sight but other cars, they came off the top of a long rise and spread before them, perhaps 10 miles away, was a pencil line of red, yellow, and green, blazing along the horizon ahead of them, a bizarre Coney Island in the middle of death and sterility; he wanted to see it, go to the gambling places, drink, but his daughter's sickness upset him, terribly, more than he cared to admit to himself—because he blamed himself for her infection, blamed himself for his children's bewilderment, his guilt was heavy on him—his wife, on the other hand, simply forgot, absolutely forgot her daughter the moment she saw those lights. Her daughter was sick, well, could she help her if she stayed with her all night any more than if she went out? That was her uncomplicated reasoning. He envied her, his own guilt swung into him so much more easily, entered his life at every moment, he tended to blame himself for every sour and unhappy look his children wore from the very moment that they had been born.

They moved into the streets of the town, a storm, a wilderness of lights, every color, all moving, a Times Square of unbelievable vulgarity, unbelievable vapidity and greed. The people walking the streets were corpses, they moved along to some distant drummer who was a psychopath, it seemed. Were they really alive—the neon on their faces turned them blue, white, red, they moved from one end of the main street to the other, back and forth, waiting for the machines to blow up and shower them with gold. And at each end of the town, blackness, death, the howling wind off the Mojave bringing tons of red dust into the streets. If for one moment, he thought, the town stopped, turned its back, the desert would pounce, Vegas would be buried under tons of clay and cactus.

They got a motel, a "normal" motel, instead of those that sold handball games, swimming pools, and baby-sitters. And while his wife looked through her wardrobe, he and the driver went back downtown to get some food for supper. In a small luncheonette, they were amazed to find that they sold corned beef, pastrami, salami, rolled beef, French fries, pickled green tomatoes—a delicatessen menu, and they bought a bagful of food, took it back, and ate on the floor, the children delighted, his daughter beginning to smile now, the pain alleviated to the extent that it was simply, dully there. His wife was dressed in a blue sheath and black stockings, high heels, and she looked so desirable that he couldn't eat. He gave the other half of his sandwich to the driver. Should I drive you two to town, he said, then pick you up later? But, of course, who would look after the children while they were gone? We can walk there, his wife said, unconvinced, but he said, hell, no, you two go, I'll read a while, I don't feel so good anyway (he looked at her). His stomach had a knot in it and he felt the edge of nausea. Oh, come on, the driver said, you don't want me to take your old lady out again? With an edge of triumph, he thought, and waited, smiling like an imbecile, waited for her to say, oh, why don't you two go. I really think I should stay here with the baby, but she said nothing, and he replied, go on out, see one of those great stage shows at the Sands or something, I'll watch the kids, and give the baby her medicine, take a nap. I really don't feel well and . . . well, maybe I'll go out when you two get back, I'd like to see the goddamn place as long as we're here.

So they left, after she put the children to bed. He lay on the adjoining bed and read a paperback for an hour or so, then got up, gagging, and threw up, bile, into the toilet. He read and smoked, tried not to think of anything, tried to concentrate on the book he was reading, but it was absurd, the story was taking place in some land so far off, the people were in misery, yet he read wrong, wrong, he found himself envying their misery. He checked his watch, woke up his daughter for her medicine, kissed her, and she went back to sleep. He lay down again and read, the envy upon him again—how lucky to be running away from spies, to be trapped in a yacht wired for destruction by the Communists, to be shadowed by the most notorious gunman in the world . . . he thought how fortunate these adventurous motherfuckers were, then he was asleep.

He woke up to see her standing over him, slightly drunk, smiling and radiant. The driver was sitting in a chair, smoking, smiling. Apparently they were in the middle of sharing something funny, it had nothing to do with him. He got up then, rubbing his eyes, the book still in his hand, open. Where did you wind up? he said, realizing that they were both high, seeing now that the driver held a half-empty fifth of bourbon in his hand. Oh, she said, the Sands, it was terrific! We saw Sammy Davis, and a big show, it was really terrific, and cheap. Yeah, the driver said, it's all cheap, they want you to save your bread for gambling, so they take it easy on prices. He said, you feel like going out again? I feel pretty good now—he was lying, for as he stood, he felt a cold lump in his stomach, nausea almost made itself triumphant as he looked at the whisky in the driver's hand, imagined himself drinking it. Sure, why not, the driver said. How's the baby been? his wife said, O.K.? Fine, I gave her her medicine at 11:30, so she's almost due, she took it fine. I thought she was running a temperature for a while, but she's O.K. now, she's cool. Let me change, he said to the driver, and went in the bathroom, put on a clean pair of slacks and a sport shirt, washed his face and hands, combed his hair. When he came out, they were laughing, and drinking from the bottle, his wife's legs were crossed, his lust moved into the nausea in his stomach sharply, almost tipping the delicate balance he maintained, he felt himself gagging, and managed to smile as he did, and they looked at him, he smiled again, no, it's O.K., he said, toothpaste. How's this book, his wife said, picking up the paperback he had put on the bed. Ah, you know, he said, spine-tingling adventure as Agent Q pursues the fiendish Dr. Bananas through the war-torn ruins of East Berlin . . . she was looking at it, I'll read a while anyway. Did you gamble, he asked, no, they both said. We just saw the show, and drove around for a while, the driver said, then they went out, he saw up his wife's thighs as she threw her legs up on the bed, the driver looked too, and then they were in the car, moving downtown toward the lights.

They went to the Golden Nugget, stood at the immense bar, and the driver ordered bourbon, he ordered a Bloody Mary, something to soothe his stomach, it was jumping now, he wanted to puke, but he sipped at the drink: it was good, cold, and with plenty of vodka in it, but the first taste moved in his mouth and down his throat like a worm, he turned, leaning against the bar, looking at the room, huge, with every game possible being played, the hum of gamblers' voices a steady burden under the clink of glasses. How you feel now, the driver asked, turning to order another bourbon. O.K., he said, except that my stomach is a little queasy . . . he belched, wetly, a backwash of tomato juice and pastrami rushed into his mouth and he swallowed it, blinking at the acridity. I'm going to try the blackjack, he said, what the fuck. He put his drink down, turned to the little booth where they changed cash into silver dollars, you want some money, he asked the driver, but he smiled, and shook his head no, I'll watch from here, I'm not lucky. He got 20 silver dollars and walked over to the nearest blackjack table, but he wasn't used to the speed of this kind of dealing, he began to stand pat at 15 or 16, rather than gauge his chances, and, in five minutes, or a little more, he was broke, and came back to the bar . . . dropped a double saw, he said, snapping his fingers, like that. You want another drink? The driver nodded, and finished the last bit in the glass, and he, bravely, downed his Bloody Mary, ordered another. Want to go somewhere else? the driver asked, and he said, wait, let me see how this drink makes me feel, and began on it but it was the same, sickening, the drink had a vague smell of fish oil, he thought, but he drank, Jesus! What is this, he thought, what the hell am I sick about, she'll be O.K., she's sleeping, they came back right away, they saw the show at the Sands, did they? What were they doing out, there are a million motels in this burg, no questions asked, you got the bread, three hours is plenty of time . . . and dressed like that, why, anybody . . . he thought again, of her, how he wanted her to come to him, simmering with lust, asking him to do the impossible, give it to me, give it to me, don't stop! Like in the books, the smooth nylon behind her knees . . . he put the drink down, I've got to split, he said, and he was smiling, as he picked up his change, rushed to the street; just outside the door he heaved, the fluid spattering his shoes and cuffs, red, red and sweet, like blood, his blood on the street, scarlet in the neon lights, and the corpses, moving by, moving around him like water, some smiling, some disgusted, he felt the driver's hand on his arm, and thought, leave her alone, you fuck, leave her alone, nutless bastard, and then they were in the car and going back to the motel, he was covered with a layer of greasy sweat, cold, and the cigarette he smoked tasted like straw, I'm sorry, man, he said, I just got fucked up with something, maybe something we ate, Christ knows.

At the motel, the driver went to his cabin, and he went into theirs, his wife was asleep. He was weak and sick, exhausted, sitting on the bed, he felt dizzy, and he pulled off his clothes slowly, laboriously, crawled under the blankets, shivering, and closed his eyes. A moment later, she was close to him, her hand was down at his groin, she was kissing his face, his forehead, and he looked at her face, a whitish blur in the dark, I'm sick, he said, I'm sick, I can't . . . and it was true, he had vomited his desire out on the streets, it was mixed with that bloody puke, covered already with a layer of sugary sand, and he said, again, I'm sick, and his penis felt like a sausage, dead and limp, sausage meat, by Dunderbeck's machine, and all the rats and pussycats will never more be seen, they'll all be ground to sausage meat in Dunderbeck's machine. She turned away from him, angry, heaving herself around, and he wondered why she should come to him, although he knew, he didn't want to know, but he knew, so changed knowledge into wondering, duped himself, second by second, as he fell asleep, that he was curious, and over all, a feeling of revenge so brittle, but revenge anyway, now you know how I feel, he thought, for once, you know how I feel. The futility of his place, with her, was intolerable, and he thought of her, begging him for impossibly lewd sensations, but he was cold, icy sweat ran from his armpit down along his rib cage, he was ground to sausage meat. Dunderbeck, oh Dunderbeck. How could you be so mean?

New York, New York

After his mother died, he worked for another three or four months, then quit his job, and relaxed. It was pleasant for a while to do nothing, wait to see what would happen to him, buy clothes, whisky, pay off all the gnawing debts they had contracted: and to be able to sit

over coffee in the morning, read the paper, then take a walk, sit outside in the back yard in the afternoons and read, stay up late at night
to read again, watch the late movie. He felt, for a while, closer to his
wife, but, then, after a while, he was in the way, he got on her nerves,
the children got on his nerves, he got into the habit of correcting her
when he thought she had done something wrong with them—and,
too, he noticed, again, that she was as sloppy as ever, as careless with
the housework. What the hell did she do all day that she couldn't
wash and wax the floors, dust the furniture? She sat, so often, in a
kind of trance, or talked on the phone for hours with girls she knew
from a drama class she rather desultorily had attended. It was to one
of these girls' houses they went one night, to a housewarming party.
It was over on the lower East Side, near Avenue B. She was just a
girl, really, perhaps 16 or 17, and they came in, he was delighted they
had gone out, it was good to be at a party, his wife seemed especially
pretty, and there was a lot of booze and beer there, and some old
friends came also, at his invitation. Drinking, drinking, he was,
then, very drunk, how hot the night was, and he stripped his shirt
off, was dancing with girls, ripe and beautiful, one particularly, in a
tight dress, long blond hair, it was a good party, and the sweat ran
down in streams from his neck and chest, his khakis were soaked at
the beltline. Then he was in the kitchen with the hostess, a sweet
young girl, albeit too theatrical, who stroked his back, saying, you're
sweating. He pushed her against the refrigerator and kissed her, she
responded quickly to him, he was overwhelmed, she wanted him,
could it be true, she wanted him! He led her out the kitchen door to
the hall, then up the stairs between their floor, the top, and the roof.
They sat on the steps, and he kissed her again, she was moaning and
kissing him passionately, she was just a child, he thought, she's a kid,
but didn't stop, rather, moved his hand up under her skirt, up her
thighs, then, she was pushing at his hand, but still kissing him, he
tried to guide her hand to his aching phallus, and did, then, and she
pulled away, she was startled, but, still, kissed him, then suddenly
he heard his wife's voice, she was at the bottom of the flight of stairs,
scowling, she was furious, take me home now, she said, take me

home, right now, and he smiled at her drunkenly, he really couldn't put anything together in his head, he had no idea why she wanted to go home, it was still early. The girl had got up and walked down the stairs to his wife, not looking at her, then into the apartment, and he followed down, get my shirt, he said. He was angry now, what the hell did she want to go home for? It was still so early. Inside the apartment his wife went for his shirt and he waited, chatting with friends, who all seemed to him rather ridiculously solemn. His wife brought the shirt and they left, but two or three people came with them and on the way to the subway, they all stopped in Tompkins Square and sang corny songs. His wife wouldn't speak to him, but then, on the way home, she put his hand in hers, and laid her head on his shoulder. We should have taken a goddamn cab, he said. He still didn't know why she should be so angry with him, he was only kidding around . . . she was just a child, did she think he was going to fuck her on the stairs? But, he thought, I guess it is a shock to her, she's been good to me, and she's pretty, guys are always coming on to her, and she's straight. I'm sorry, baby, he said, then stroked her hair, her cheek, I'm sorry. She looked at him, and her eyes were full of tears. When they got home, he stripped her gently on the couch and they gently made love, she wept as he held her close to him after, what a son of a bitch he was, he thought. They slept in each other's arms.

Mojave Desert

Just across this most grim and parched area, and they would be in Bakersfield, and then up the beautiful Central Valley to San Francisco. So, it was just a question of this one day of driving, and tonight they would stay in California, see green, it would be warm. The desert, even now, however, seemed to raise the temperature, it was difficult to imagine that a few days back they had been caught in a fierce snowstorm in New Mexico, and almost frozen in the bitter cold air of the Grand Canyon park. Here, it was sunny, warm, they drove with the windows open, once saw a lake, and it became a mirage, it was really a mirage, fading and finally disappearing as they approached it. Toward midafternoon, the air became heavy with sand as they rode into wind, and, slowly, the sun was blotted out until it sat in the sky, tiny and as silver as the moon, a reddish, choking haze spread over everything. They passed half-finished and abandoned housing developments in the middle of nothing, with names like Desert Acres, and Sunny Sands, blistered raw wood skeletons pushing through the choking dust, spooky in the unearthly light that covered the world.

His daughter seemed to have got over her throat infection completely, her earache was gone and her temperature down to normal. She was looking out the window while he sat in the back with her and his son; he was teaching him the piece moves with an old chess set they had brought along, but the strange light and the dust storm had ended their game and now they stared up at the old dime that the sun had become, he felt all right, he somehow felt exonerated now, after last night, his refusal. She and the driver chatted and laughed in the front seat, they seemed close together, a warmth existed between them, stronger, it seemed to him, than friendship, they talked with him and the children continually, she seemed to have forgotten about last night, not annoyed, nor vindictive. His guilt flowed away with her steady ignoring of the facts, and he was pleased, it was better to be so, even the children sensed an air of lightness about them. But mostly perhaps it was because the trip was almost over, tomorrow they would be in San Francisco, seeing old friends, Christmas would be truly an occasion for celebration, stability, there would be presents and to spare to make up to the children for this long trip, the lack of their own home in which to spend the day.

Toward the end of the afternoon it got brighter, since they were moving out of the desert, as such, into higher ground, they rose steadily, almost imperceptibly, where there had been a few cacti, scattered, before, they now grew in clumps, huge, almost lush-looking, and they saw, on occasion, patches of green in the distance . . .

it seemed to him that he hadn't seen grass (could it be grass?) in years. Near the top of a long, circling, climbing road, they came around a dome-shaped hill, and dropping off below them, to their right, was a sloping valley, brilliant green with grass, dotted with black-and-white cows, grazing. It was unbelievably beautiful, a sense of vitality possessed him at once, the grass, the cows were indicative of life, and there were houses in the distance, and farm machinery . . . it was soft and burnished, the scene, in the gentle late afternoon light, all the angles of the landscape softened, the grass startling in its brightness; cows lifted their heads occasionally at the traffic, and lowed. They kept climbing, then saw signs for Bakersfield, Fresno, Madera, Merced; they seemed magic names to him, the dryness past, the great Central Valley was just over this last chain of innocuous hills, it was warm and green, fertile with fruits and grapes, the desert lay behind them, tortured and frenzied in wind and dust, sterility gripped it at this very moment that he sat, smiling, his head half out the window in the perfumed air, pointing at the cows and barns for his children, the lights of Bakersfield beginning to go on in the bluish dusk far below them at the mouth of the valley.

Bakersfield, California

He was disappointed when they finally rode into the streets of Bakersfield, because by that time the sun had gone down, and he hungered for the sight of trees and grass. It was beautiful, though, to smell the rich, fertile odor of arable soil, borne to them through the open windows of the car. Everyone was delighted, and now too, they were not forced to stop at the first motel they saw for the night, there were towns ahead, dozens of them, and they could drive for a couple of hours, stop whenever they felt the children were too tired. They decided to eat at a drive-in and move on to Fresno or Madera before taking a place for the night. He wanted them to get as close to San Francisco as they could this night, so that the next day would find

them in town in the early afternoon, but, at the same time, he wanted
to see as much as he could of this rich valley by sunlight. Fresno or
Madera would bring them halfway to San Francisco, and the plan
seemed fine to him, and to the others. They hadn't eaten in a drive-
in since they had been in the Midwest, and the children were, as
then, delighted. They ordered the usual hamburgers, French fries,
all the trimmings, and cokes and beer. It was a great pleasure to eat,
the windows rolled down, cars and people passing, the sound of life
around them, instead of that wind-filled silence of the desert. He
realized how dependent he was on the city, feared, as he had feared
secretly since the beginning, what isolation in a small Mexican vil-
lage might do to him, could he stand it, for a year even? But for now,
he was pleased, felt that somehow they had made it, a sense of
triumph pervaded him. His wife ordered a third hamburger and he
and the driver joked about her appetite, and he said that maybe he'd
let the driver take her off his hands, with *that* appetite. He laughed,
as did the driver, but she smiled, looked at him strangely, almost
frightened, then at the driver. Outside the edge of the strained
laughter, and the quick banter which followed it, there was a lurking,
ominous silence, waiting to invade the car when the talk died: but
they would not allow it, talked quickly and lightly, until there was no
longer any need to, then paid the check, and moved out onto the
road, heading northwest toward Fresno, the radio on. They even got
some jazz, for the first time since leaving New York.

New York, New York

It was just like any other party he had been to since returning. He
was drunk, they had run out of ice. He drank the bourbon mixed
with water that was none too cold. Things seemed sharply faceted.
One of the men who had been among his wife's lovers was there, and
they spoke, carefully, they both knew, he loathed himself for not
having even the desire to punch him when he first found out, some
weeks before, now it was too late, so, they spoke, civilized. The man

was drunk too, there with a woman who was married, she was some sort of schoolteacher, she didn't seem to belong here with these manic and bitter painters and poets, gay or grim in their varying degrees of success or failure. She was white and extraordinarily taken with the fact that her lover was a Negro, it somehow seemed very important to her.

There was loud music, it was very loud, time had certainly passed, and the loft was crowded now, there was ice in his glass, and everybody was drunk, some passed out, one puking in the sink. He was talking to a girl, listening very hard to what she was saying, it seemed to be something about herself, her life, what she thought she should do. She was pretty, well dressed, though by now he was so drunk he really didn't know if she was or not, and slowly he realized that ten or a dozen people had formed a loose semicircle and were looking at the Negro who was now dancing with his girl, they were clapping and cheering, and he looked then. They weren't dancing, really, he was simply throwing her around, now he threw her over his back, she slid over him, laughing, manic now as the audience, one of her shoes flew off and he wrestled her, biting her neck, he was sweating and laughing, it was fearful laughter, edged like a knife, it wasn't at all funny. He stared at them, perplexed, he was uncertainly angry, looking at her, a smile that really was just a fixed grimace on her face, her eyes blank with fright and humiliation, she looked up at everybody as he threw her to the floor, and she said, oh, and he grabbed her ankles, her skirt up around her thighs, he looked away, embarrassed, then looked back, she was in the same position, he was sliding her back and forth on the floor like a wheelbarrow and everybody was laughing, the women harder than the men, they acted as if somehow they were winning something. His hands closed over hers then and he lifted her, pulled her taut across his back again, her stockings were lined with runs, the seat of her skirt was filthy, and she was crying now, yelling his name, over and over, then she was on her hands and knees looking for her shoe, the Negro was standing alone, swaying, looking around, laughing uproariously, then he looked over at the husband, his eyes were triumphant, people were laughing harder now, he wasn't sure at whom, he drank his whisky and felt it trickle, then gush down his chin, his neck, soak his collar. He turned away, fumbling for his handkerchief, pushing through walls of laughter.

Madera, California

It was late when they got into Madera, the traffic had been heavier than they expected, the children were sleeping in the back. The weather had so suddenly turned warm that they all felt drowsy, the winy smell of the vineyards, too, acted as a soporific. They chose the first motel they saw, and checked in, within the hour the children had been bathed and put to bed, and soon after, he and his wife were asleep, the driver in an adjoining room. He dreamed of his mother, she was chasing him, bouncing along a road, sunny, which led through a red desert, she journeyed on a pogo stick, he ran furiously but each bound brought her to within inches of his back, he could make no gain at all, and she held out a fistful of money to him, silently, her face was that of the woman in the coffin, calm and painted, bloated, and he sweated in fear, why did she chase him, she was dead: he awoke suddenly, heard in a moment his wife breathing beside him and got out of bed, lit a cigarette. He put on his shoes, shirt, and pants and walked outside, the night was heavy and black, just behind their cabin ran a narrow dirt road, and he walked to it, stood on it, an aromatic cat's paw caressed him. Bordering the road were acres of vineyards, massed and clumped together in the darkness, the crisp sound of their leaves quiet and soothing to him. He smoked, walked aimlessly back and forth on the road, San Francisco tomorrow, he thought, and then we'll see what will happen with us. He tossed the cigarette away, and walked back to the cabin, let himself in quietly, undressed and lay down again. He thought of his dead garden, the peach trees cut down, and missed it all with intense sharpness. If they hadn't built that fucking house we would have stayed, he thought, we would have stayed and everything would have been O.K. What he meant by O.K. was that everything would have remained in its long-ago attained state of rot, but it would have been submerged rot. He needed, however, the monumentally trite fable of the good old days to avoid their drab truth, in his heart he suspected, even, that the time would come when he would speak, and perhaps even think, of this trip as fun, as adventure, this very moment would become part of the good old days.

Central Valley, California

It was a beautiful valley, now, in the morning sun, Biblical remembrances of a land of milk and honey seemed to find reality in the countryside around them; everywhere were citrus groves, vineyards, farms of all kinds; and everywhere, too, battered cars and trucks carrying migrants, both white and Mexican, bent in the sunlight, their eyes fixed on the road ahead, they had no share at all in this fecundity, existed, simply, to labor in it, pallid and pasty with lack of food and vitamins, they moved toward the next two- or three-day job.

They were north of Madera now, and along the road, every three or four miles, saw orange-juice stands, where juice was sold in huge containers, over cracked ice, for 35¢, the stands glittered white and orange in the sun, atop many of them a giant plaster orange as advertisement, behind them, stretching away to the horizon, orange groves, the fruit heavy on the trees, the ground littered with broken and rotting oranges, a thin, sweet smell of juice in the air. Past Merced and Modesto, and they would be in San Francisco within an hour or two, perhaps about three in the afternoon, how strange it would be to sit down until after the new year, three weeks or more in an old friend's house, how long now, he thought. It was at least four years since W and his wife and son had moved here, to "get away from New York." And all they spoke of in letters was how much they wanted to come back, how much they missed the noise and dirt, missed, especially, the change of seasons. Were they all right, he wondered, how was their marriage . . . she couldn't have changed much from the dull-witted poseur she had always been, her maddening volume of Proust on her lap for what must have been three years, slogging through those myopic pages, and W, sitting there looking at her, *yes dear, no dear,* a look of amused malice on his face, the drooling child of another man sitting there, running there, how was he? Would they really be glad to see them, that bothered him. All the letters had been full of joy at the news that they were journeying west, how delighted to see them they'd be, plenty of room, and the rest. We'll see, he thought, but did not worry . . . they had money— *I* have money, he thought—and if it's rotten, a hotel will do fine, just to stay in one spot, though, till Christmas is over, let the children have a tree, presents, and the rest. To give them, finally, after this month of travel, respite . . . and they could play with the kid.

They were past Merced now, the signs were most decidedly urban along the road, highways merged, crossed, the traffic was heavy toward the north, soon they would be there, God, how he wanted to see W again, get drunk with him, and laugh, what good friends they had been! Perhaps his wife, too, would be able to talk to that stupid ass, perhaps there was some obvious methodology of maintenance in marriage that she, in spite of her vapidity, knew. At once, he was delighted that they would be there, and terrified that now the trip, except for the permanence of the final settling in Mexico, was over. And if she did decide to leave . . . and with him . . . ? He looked at the driver, his mustache bushy now, his sunglasses blank dark on the road ahead, and the early feeling that he was a complete stranger who moved them as he wished came over him, and again, who is he? Why did he come? They were entering the city limits of Modesto and decided to stop for lunch, the children wanted orange juice, the huge brilliant oranges atop the roadside stands were too much for them.

San Francisco, California

He thought that the bridge they approached was the Golden Gate, but it was the Bay Bridge, and then they were on it, over the bay, the sunlight glittering on the small waves far below. His feeling was one of triumph now, they had come to the sea, he wanted to see it, he

could smell the salt, the gentle air was filled with it, the people had
the quicker motions, the vitality he had always assumed to be a
concomitant of living near the ocean. They were over the bridge
now, and in San Francisco, asking directions to W's house, moving
through afternoon streets, then alongside a small park, actually a
series of large, grassy traffic islands with benches and trees, he
looked and looked for signs of poverty, anywhere, could this be a
large city, everyone seemed to be so well off, and W had told him,
even, that he lived in a working-class neighborhood, he himself
worked for a newspaper in the classified-ads department. They
found the street easily enough, after one false alarm that brought
them up a fantastic hill, at its crest, the city spread below them, other
hills smooth and mellow in the sun, clumps of wooden houses
blurred in whites and pastels, the whole curved around a bright
green sea, he could make out churnings of whitecaps placed sporad-
ically on the brilliant green of the water. It was the most beautiful
city he had ever seen.

W lived in the middle of the block, and they parked the car, neighbors stared as they got out, and then he rang the bell, holding his
son's hand, and heard her voice come down the stairs, and answered,
and she ran down, embraced him, his wife, the children smiled uncertainly, the driver smiled, carrying in bags. It was a nice apartment, it was exciting to be here now, and she dialed her husband's
number at work, told him excitedly that they had arrived, and he
said he would leave immediately. They sat and talked, talked about
the city, old friends, and she made drinks for them, he felt himself
getting drunk, he was expansive, he was rich, he would buy booze,
food, what a great visit it would be. He was, really, happy. When W
came in, the husband was so moved at seeing him again that he felt
on the edge of tears, they embraced, and the talk started again, the
boy was home from school now, and the three children sized up each
other, he heard W's boy boast about his prowess in school, that he
was on a football team, he asked his son if he could read, and he said,
almost, and the kid pulled out a school reader and demonstrated his
abilities, his son was embarrassed, and then W walked over and tore

the book from his son's hand, said, not now, stupid, the child looked at him, his mouth hanging open dully, there was a kind of brutality on the boy's face, not his fault. The husband looked at him, and felt ashamed that he should think this, but his thoughts switched instantly as they resumed talking again, and went out, then, for liquor, the walk was quiet, W asked him who the driver was, and he knew that he meant *why* the driver, moved swiftly into his pat explanation, lack of a license, the man's knowledge of Mexico, and so forth. The subject was changed, and he was grateful.

Later, he would think of all the time in San Francisco as a series of events which were logically linked together, one necessary for that one which followed, at the time, however, they were discrete, chaotic, the stay at W's house, as they waited for Christmas, became extremely uncomfortable, they were, after the first 5 days or so, not welcome. Their son was, indeed, a boor and a bully, and delighted in baiting his children, being cruel to them as behooved the rightful occupant of the house, the rightful owner of the toybox. W was either tired, or drunk, or both, when he got home from work, and his resentment over the fact that he was working at a steady job while his guests slept late, drove around town, drank and shopped, was accumulative, the wife seemed simply grasping, and each day asked him for what seemed to be an extraordinary amount of money for groceries for all of them; this annoyed him, since he had spent roughly fifty dollars on liquor and wine since they had arrived, and W and she drank as much, or more of it, than they did. Another friend, from college, lived here with his wife, now pregnant, and they saw them on occasion, they were genuinely delighted that they were here, and asked them continually to come and stay at their place for the remainder of their visit. There was an unspoken understanding concerning the tension and apathy in W's house.

One day, a day that would remain with him, it seemed later, forever, he sat at home alone with his son, teaching the boy how to read. He had decided that he would begin this teaching earlier, but had not, until now, a chance. Now, however, since they were to be settled for a while, he decided to begin, particularly since W's son so delighted in annoying his son with his capabilities. They had been at it an hour, the house was quiet, everybody else out, shopping downtown for Christmas decorations, when the boy came in from school. Immediately the lesson faltered as the boy looked over his shoulder, read easily the words that his son was trying to spell out, laboriously. A fury gripped him and he wanted to smash at the child, grasp him and shake him, but he held himself in, almost sweetly said, that's enough for now, to his son. The two children went into the boy's room and he sat on the couch and tried to read, but couldn't. It was impossible for him to believe that it was near Christmas, the sun was warm and springlike, the quiet was lazy, scattered voices and sounds came from the street below. He heard the argument then, and, in a moment, his son came into the living room, almost in tears: it was the old story again, the boy refused to let him play with any of his toys, wanted him to stand there, empty-handed, and watch *him* play; and, following the pattern of the last week or so exactly, he followed his son into the living room, pouting and angry in a gross, almost mature ugliness—he wanted to savor his son's tears, it didn't fit his plans at all that he should leave him to play, alone, with toys he had long lost interest in. You wanna fight, he said to his son, and put up his fists. God, how he hated this child, and then, maliciously, he decided that he would let them fight, he would "guide" them in a boxing lesson, hoping that he could so arrange it that his son could hurt W's boy, hurt him, under the guise of playfulness; and he would be there to see that his son wasn't hurt at all. A tank job, he thought, and smiled, how about learning to box, you kids, and, of course, the boy said, I can box, I can box better than anybody, and swung his arms wildly, fiercely, at his son. The husband shook his head in false patience, made them stand together, noticed that his son was unhappy about this, didn't at all want to have anything to do with this boy. There was a vulgarity about him that his son had never experienced, the child was emotionally poor, he was really blinded to love. But his son did as he told him to, and he showed them how to put their hands up, guard themselves, jab, cross, and move. He started them fighting then, exhorting them to hit at each other with their

palms, not fists, and they began, the boy swinging wildly, with, as he
had guessed, his fists, striking his son on the forearms, repeatedly.
He stood behind his son, directing him, but his son was loath to
strike his opponent, he didn't really understand the violence so manifest in the other boy, but the husband prodded him, now angry that
his son was being hit, constantly, on the arms, the chest, the other
boy was trying to hit him in the face, and the husband was screaming
at him now to open his fists, his anger was so great, his anger and
frustration so acute that he clenched his fist and would have punched
the child with all his strength had he not thought, stop, you stupid
son of a bitch, and he continued prodding his son, showing him
openings, while his son followed his direction, stoically, his arms red
from the wild blows that rained on them, the other boy heeding
nothing, merely feeling the triumph of hitting, punching, landing
blows. It was no longer a game, the three of them knew it, he was
committed to it now, committed to it for his own sake, as well as his
son's, and then, beautifully, his son shot in a jab as the other boy
lunged in swinging, the hand shot through between his arms and the
slap was loud and crisp in the room. His son looked up at him, he was
frightened that he had hit the other boy, and the other boy was furious, raging, swinging, his fists balled, punching insanely at the
arms that stuck out in front of him, and, he, now, pushed the boy
back, shouted, no fists, goddammit! No fists! and now his son was
crying, and he said, you're doing fine, champ, get another one of
those jabs in there, he can't touch you, laughing, his heart in his
mouth, bitter, and he felt nauseous, his son crying silently, his arms
crimson and swollen, following his instructions, dancing about,
pushing his hands forward doggedly, each time receiving the other
boy's punches without saying a word, uttering a sound. His son was
struck then, in the chest, and fell backward, looked at his father,
tried to smile, then burst out in tears, and the husband stopped the
fight, O.K., that's enough, he said, that's enough. He was chewing
on his tongue, the tears were drowning his eyes and he wiped viciously at them, turned then to the other boy, you'll never learn how
to fight, he said, you know why, because you're stupid, you're stupid

and you won't listen. But the other boy laughed, and jumped up and down, laughing, I won, he said, I won! You little bastard! he screamed then, and raised his hand, then dropped it, and smiled, nobody *won* anything. I was trying to teach you guys how to box. He put his arm around his son's shoulders, you learn quick, champ, he said, his heart breaking, while the other boy jumped up and down, ran, then, into his room, calling, I'm gonna play with my soldiers. He led his son into the bathroom and washed his swollen, red arms with cold water, dried his tears, and sat there, on the edge of the tub, holding him close, filled with a shame so loathsome, so filthy, that he shivered. What about a soda, he said . . . for the champ? His son smiled at him, and he led him out, down the stairs, and around the corner to an ice-cream parlor. Oh God, forgive me, he thought, forgive me, my baby.

He sat at home with the children and W's wife during the afternoon of Christmas Eve, while the driver and his wife went out to buy him a surprise present—he had insisted that it was silly to buy him a present, but they said they wanted to, and he was moved to a small degree, when the driver told him that he had saved some money for the express purpose of chipping in for the gift; so they left, and he began to drink. There was an uneasy truce in the house between him and W's wife, as there was between his children and her son, so they sat in silence, she sewed, and, after he put the tree on its stand, he sat again, continued to drink, and read—the children played, somehow, in the boy's room, miraculously without tears or arguments. W would be home from work early, she said, and then they could all trim the tree together. He dreaded this job, as he really dreaded everything about Christmas and the holiday season. It served merely to conjure up to him the memory of his childhood, Christmas with a "family" which exchanged presents without laughter or warmth, the wrapping paper put carefully away, immediately, then one highball, and bed, as usual. Ever since he had been old enough to find excuses to be out of the house on Christmas Eve he had gone, each time drinking himself blind with anybody he could find in a bar, or bars—

there was a fellowship in them that had never existed in his home, it was absurd, but the old terror of the holidays remained with him, and he drank steadily, stiff bourbon highballs, plenty of ice and a minimum of water. What time will the breadwinner be home, did you say? and she said, oh, he'll probably stop for a few drinks first with the people from the office but he should be home around 4 or so—there's no party or anything, but she was afraid, he knew, in a sense, she was convinced that he would stagger home late, drunk, sodden, and fall into bed.

His wife and the driver got home about 4:30, mysterious with their gay package, and he was good and drunk by now, tried his best to show interest in their secret, attempting to peek, trying to guess— all the claptrap that he had learned over the years. W's wife was annoyed at all this, and this pleased him, for he had the idea (and was right) that his drunkenness simply reminded her of her husband, not yet home, and he couldn't resist asking, maybe we should start the tree without him? and she glared at him, then spoke to his wife and the driver as if he hadn't said a word: he nodded, and made himself another drink. It was after 6 when W reeled in, valiantly trying to look as if he had just a slight Christmas glow on, but he was smashed, the banal lipstick all over his collar and lapels, what a delight! He poured himself half a tumbler of whisky, and when his wife asked him if he had had a good time, dear, he said, I don't remember anything, and giggled, then turned on the radio and began drinking with his old friend, good old buddy, do you remember the time when.

And so the evening passed, the driver putting the decorations on the tree, helped by his wife and W's, while they sat, giving directions, a sword-edge of ill-feeling over everything, terrific! Just like old times, good old X-mas! Only the driver didn't care, he went along with their banter, and drank, as they did, he didn't care, he was a fucking chameleon, the husband thought . . . and three hours to get me a present, I know what you bastards were up to . . . but he didn't care about that either. The rest of the evening passed, he recalled his wife and W's whispering to each other in the kitchen, each time he went to get more ice, they were whispering, they were both crying, that's all women can do, anyway, whisper and cry, merry Christmas, go fuck yourself, said Tiny Tim! Hilarious! He and W laughed for hours over things they had done years ago in Brooklyn, grim enough at the time, now glittering with nostalgia— and the papers said that New York was choked with snow, he had tears in his eyes. This goddamn town is lousy, no snow, all this goddamn grass, why don't you come back to New York, kid, he said, but W was snoring in the chair, his glass knocked over, the whisky staining the rug. He sat and squinted at the driver. I hope you got me a nice present, he said. What is it, maybe a nice gearshift, a nice clutch . . . maybe a ring job? He staggered to the couch and fell asleep.

Brooklyn, New York

He was delighted because his mother asked him if he'd like French fries for supper, and he loved French fries. The house was cold and he and she sat in the kitchen, the oven on to warm them. His grandfather had been over, brought a little artificial tree, the decorations permanently attached to it, and it was set in the living room. His mother peeled the potato, sliced it, and pan-fried it, served it to him with ketchup, and bread and margarine. The whole potato? he said, mom? The whole potato for me, don't you want any? She said, no, son, I'm not hungry, you eat it, I'll have a sandwich later, after you go to sleep and Santa comes. He finished the potato, then poured ketchup on a piece of bread and made a sandwich, ate it with tea. His mother put him to bed, and he fell asleep, thinking of Santa, and electric trains, except that his mother said that electric trains only went to boys in the country because in the city they had the subway. It must be true, none of his friends had trains. He woke up in the night, and heard a noise in the living room, sneaked to the door to catch Santa, and saw his mother placing a little metal pig, dressed in a sailor suit, under the tree. The pig had a drum, and then he saw his mother sit on the couch and begin to cry. He wondered why the tree didn't have any lights, and he wondered why his mother had put the pig under the tree—he hadn't asked for a pig, that was for babies. And why was she crying? Well, Santa wasn't here yet. In the morning, the pig stared at him, and he picked it up, wound it with the key sticking out of its blue jumper. He put it down, and it bounced and clattered on the linoleum spastically, pounding on the tin drum. He couldn't understand why he had this pig, and why Santa hadn't come, after all . . . he *hadn't* come, because his mother had put the pig under the tree. And why was she crying? The pig skittered to a stop and fell over, and he saw his mother in the doorway, do you like your present, son? she said. Yes, he said, winding it up again. It would take him a long time to figure this out. Who wants a toy pig?

San Francisco, California

Christmas was over, uneventful, although Q and his wife had come over, and some other friends whom they had known in New York, now San Francisco residents. They had had a good dinner, eggnog, all the rest, and, although he had paid for everything, he felt all right. What the hell. His wife and the driver had got him a desk pen, with stand, on which was a gold plaque for his initials. They hadn't had time to do that, they said. He didn't care, it was obvious that the gift had been bought with the minimum of effort, much as one might buy a bottle of milk. One thing pleased him, though. He had arranged with Q and his wife that they would leave W's house the next morning, the day after Christmas, and spend their remaining week or so at their place before going on to Mexico . . . it was impossible here, he said, and didn't say, she's charging me about 50 bucks a week, exclusive of booze. W went to bed early, his wife hungrily following him, the tension between them salient. He and his wife and the driver talked quietly, there was a strange feeling of separation in the air, he was certain now that they were up to something, but still . . . he couldn't be sure, why would they bother to make the change to Q's house if they were up to anything, why not just come out with it, now? He didn't care, he told himself.

The next morning, they piled everything in the car, telling W's wife at the last minute that they decided to take advantage of Q's hospitality, since his house was bigger, it would be better for everybody. Surprisingly, she was angry and acted as if Q had done something unforgivable in inviting them to stay with him, but he couldn't be worried about it, they were on their way, the car packed with their belongings, supplemented with Christmas presents now. Q did have a huge place, and they made sleeping arrangements, even the children had a room to themselves, and Q borrowed two old cots from a friend so that they would be comfortable. By the time everything was settled, it was late and his wife fed the children, after which he played tiddlywinks with them for a half hour, then put them to bed. His son said, I'm glad we came here, dad, I didn't like it there, I didn't like that boy at all. I know, he said, well, we'll be here for a while, and you won't have to play with him any more, or sleep in the room with him, just you and your sister. He said good night, and then the five adults sat around with a couple of nightcaps, talking about W and his wife, about what had happened to them in the past year, the great change that seemed to come over them when they found out that she couldn't have any more children. So they're stuck with just him, he thought, and it's not even W's. The warmth of the room was rich and soothing, the fireplace crackled genially, and he felt good again, the tension of living with them drained out of him with the passing moments. In a very real sense, however, he was grateful for those tensions, it was the first time in weeks that they had been caused by something other than his wife, their half-life together on this trip. Now, he began to think of her again. She seemed relaxed, sure of herself, smiling. She kept glancing over at him as if she wanted to talk to him, her eyes were pleading, and when she said, well, I'm tired, I'm going to bed, he stood up too, finished his drink, and said, I'm knocked out, myself, and looked at her. She seemed relieved, grateful, and his heart pounded with desire and hope as he

brushed his teeth, then came out to say good night, enter the bedroom which Q had given them as guest room. She was in bed and he
switched the light off and undressed, slid into bed, trembling with
excitement. She wanted him, he knew, he knew it! She had invited
him to come to bed with her for the first time in—baby, he said,
embracing her, oh, baby, it's going to be all right. I don't love you
any more, she said. He listened to the words, continued to embrace
her, baby, he said, we . . . I don't, she said, I'm going to leave you.
He released her and leaned on an elbow, peered at her face, pale in
the dark. He knew it would come, but, now? After she had invited
him to bed? Whatever world he had constructed over the past few
years, shored up over the past weeks of the trip, had numerous escape routes, safety valves: he had long known all this, had even prepared himself for it, but this was simply insanity, tonight . . . and
why did he come here, why did she come here, why not tell him over
at W's house? Who, he said, who? The great friend, our guide and
scout? Oh, please, she said, and turned from him. How long, he said,
how long have you known about it? We decided that day—when we
bought your present. Did you fuck him, he said, hah? Did you two
fuck? He was furious now, not so much at the fact that he knew they
had, but because of the fact that he couldn't. That day, she said, we
went to a motel. And before? On the trip? In Las Vegas, she said.
Before? Shhh, she said. Before! he said, goddammit, where. In New
Orleans, she said. He was festering in his hatred now, he wanted her
and she was laying for that assless filth, that bastard, while he ate his
food and drank his booze, and he couldn't fuck her at all. This is
monstrous, he thought, behind his screen of abuse, because he knew
that it was true that his fury was not at all because she had done this
with the driver, but that she hadn't done it with him. Now, though,
things were changed, she was leaving. Where will you go? We can go
to San Antonio, that friend of his will give him a job with his drug
company. And then you can fuck the friend, too. They were silent,
and he smoked. He felt a fantastic freedom, but a sense of futility
that negated any pleasure such a feeling bestowed. You better be
good to those children, he said, you whore. I was right about you, all

the time, before we got married, down at the pier, you remember
. . . but their daughter was crying, and she got up to go to her. When
she got back, he asked, how many other guys? Everyone, she said,
for Christ's sake, everyone, you damn fool, most of your marvelous
friends! He thought then, almost hoping for her, that maybe she
really *was* in love, after all, with this man, I can't even drive, I live
on my mother's corpse, fuck it. He lay in the dark, actually worrying
about telling Q in the morning. He felt no animosity toward the
driver, merely contempt. He even decided to let them have the car,
feeling somehow superior, aloof, because of his largesse.

It wasn't until they had gone that he missed the children. The two
weeks he spent with Q and his wife were an alcoholic blur in which
he went out only to buy more whisky. Once or twice they took him
out to a movie or to North Beach and once or twice he went out
himself, with the vague intention of picking up a girl, but he felt old
and drained, and unsure of himself. He had no sexual desire at all,
and was sure she had somehow made him impotent. After 10 days he
bought a train ticket to New York, and, soon after, left.

Albuquerque, New Mexico

Before making the move to Taos, he and the driver and M drove to
Albuquerque to get a used refrigerator from a man well set up in
business there. He was a heroin addict, but wealthy, and so his habit
interfered with nothing, his wife was an alcoholic, spending her life
in bed, propped up on pillows reading mystery stories and drinking
a couple of fifths of brandy a day. They got the refrigerator on the
trailer and went back in to have a drink before they started the long
trip back to Santa Fe. The man sat in the living room, his eyes
clouded, smiling secretly. The woman weaved around the room un-
steadily, making a pitcher of Martinis, getting ice and whisky, laying
out cheeses and crackers. They sat in the twilight, fast moving in to
the room, a great rhomboid of crimson sunlight fixed on the wall

behind the man and his wife, who now sat together, hand in hand. He was eating éclairs and drinking coffee and she gulped at her Martini, then poured another. There was a momentary lull in the conversation, and he gazed at the couple. They were looking at the three guests, smiling, their eyes calm and blank, their fingers intertwined. They sat, decorous and serene, staring into the gentle sunlight, blunted, secure from each other, and from everything else.

Gilbert Sorrentino born in 1929 in Brooklyn, has published more than two dozen books of fiction, poetry and criticism, including *Mulligan Stew*, *Steelwork*, *Imaginative Qualities of Actual Things*, and *Aberration of Starlight*. He has received numerous literary prizes including the John Dos Passos Prize for Literature, two Guggenheim Fellowships, an Award for Literature from the American Academy of Arts and Letters, and a Lannan Literary Award.

DALKEY ARCHIVE PAPERBACKS

FELIPE ALFAU, *Chromos.*
  Locos.
  Sentimental Songs.
ALAN ANSEN,
  Contact Highs: Selected Poems 1957-1987.
DJUNA BARNES, *Ladies Almanack.*
  Ryder.
JOHN BARTH, *LETTERS.*
  Sabbatical.
ANDREI BITOV, *Pushkin House.*
ROGER BOYLAN, *Killoyle.*
CHRISTINE BROOKE-ROSE, *Amalgamemnon.*
GERALD BURNS, *Shorter Poems.*
MICHEL BUTOR,
  Portrait of the Artist as a Young Ape.
JULIETA CAMPOS, *The Fear of Losing Eurydice.*
ANNE CARSON, *Eros the Bittersweet.*
LOUIS-FERDINAND CÉLINE, *Castle to Castle.*
  North.
  Rigadoon.
HUGO CHARTERIS, *The Tide Is Right.*
JEROME CHARYN, *The Tar Baby.*
EMILY HOLMES COLEMAN, *The Shutter of Snow.*
ROBERT COOVER, *A Night at the Movies.*
STANLEY CRAWFORD,
  Some Instructions to My Wife.
RENÉ CREVEL, *Putting My Foot in It.*
RALPH CUSACK, *Cadenza.*
SUSAN DAITCH, *Storytown.*
PETER DIMOCK,
  A Short Rhetoric for Leaving the Family.
COLEMAN DOWELL, *Island People.*
  Too Much Flesh and Jabez.
RIKKI DUCORNET, *The Fountains of Neptune.*
  The Jade Cabinet.
  Phosphor in Dreamland.
  The Stain.

WILLIAM EASTLAKE, *Lyric of the Circle Heart.*
STANLEY ELKIN, *The Dick Gibson Show.*
ANNIE ERNAUX, *Cleaned Out.*
LAUREN FAIRBANKS, *Muzzle Thyself.*
  Sister Carrie.
LESLIE A. FIEDLER,
  Love and Death in the American Novel.
RONALD FIRBANK, *Complete Short Stories.*
FORD MADOX FORD, *The March of Literature.*
JANICE GALLOWAY, *Foreign Parts.*
  The Trick Is to Keep Breathing.
WILLIAM H. GASS,
  Willie Masters' Lonesome Wife.
C. S. GISCOMBE, *Giscome Road.*
  Here.
KAREN ELIZABETH GORDON, *The Red Shoes.*
GEOFFREY GREEN, ET AL, *The Vineland Papers.*
PATRICK GRAINVILLE, *The Cave of Heaven.*
JOHN HAWKES, *Whistlejacket.*
ALDOUS HUXLEY, *Antic Hay.*
  Point Counter Point.
  Those Barren Leaves.
  Time Must Have a Stop.
TADEUSZ KONWICKI, *The Polish Complex.*
EWA KURYLUK, *Century 21.*
OSMAN LINS,
  The Queen of the Prisons of Greece.
ALF MAC LOCHLAINN,
  The Corpus in the Library.
  Out of Focus.
D. KEITH MANO, *Take Five.*
BEN MARCUS, *The Age of Wire and String.*
DAVID MARKSON, *Collected Poems.*
  Reader's Block.
  Springer's Progress.
  Wittgenstein's Mistress.
CARL R. MARTIN, *Genii Over Salzburg.*

DALKEY ARCHIVE PAPERBACKS

Dalkey Archive Press
ISU Box 4241, Normal, IL 61790–4241
fax (309) 438–7422
Visit our website at www.cas.ilstu.edu/english/dalkey/dalkey.html